JACQUELINE WOODSON

hush

PUFFIN BOOKS
An Imprint of Penguin Group (USA) Inc.

PUFFIN BOOKS
Published by the Penguin Group
Penguin Young Readers Group, 345 Hudson Street, New York, New York 10014, U.S.A.
Penguin Group (Canada), 90 Eglinton Avenue East, Suite 700, Toronto, Ontario, Canada M4P 2Y3
(a division of Pearson Penguin Canada Inc.)
Penguin Books Ltd, 80 Strand, London WC2R 0RL, England
Penguin Ireland, 25 St Stephen's Green, Dublin 2, Ireland (a division of Penguin Books Ltd)
Penguin Group (Australia), 250 Camberwell Road, Camberwell, Victoria 3124, Australia
(a division of Pearson Australia Group Pty Ltd)
Penguin Books India Pvt Ltd, 11 Community Centre, Panchsheel Park, New Delhi - 110 017, India
Penguin Group (NZ), 67 Apollo Drive, Rosedale, North Shore 0632, New Zealand
(a division of Pearson New Zealand Ltd.)
Penguin Books (South Africa) (Pty) Ltd, 24 Sturdee Avenue,
Rosebank, Johannesburg 2196, South Africa

Registered Offices: Penguin Books Ltd, 80 Strand, London WC2R 0RL, England

First published in the United States of America by G. P. Putnam's Sons, a division of Penguin
Young Readers Group, 2002
This edition published by Puffin Books, a division of Penguin Young Readers Group, 2010

3 5 7 9 10 8 6 4

THE LIBRARY OF CONGRESS HAS CATALOGED THE G.P. PUTNAM'S SONS EDITION AS FOLLOWS:
Woodson, Jacqueline.
Hush / Jacqueline Woodson
p.   cm.
Summary: Thirteen-year-old Toswiah finds her life changes when her family enters the witness
protection program.
ISBN: 978-0-399-23114-8 (hc)
[1. Witness protection programs—Fiction. 2. African Americans—Fiction.
3. Jehovah's Witnesses—Fiction.]
I. Title.
PZ7.W868 Hu 2002 [Fic]—dc21   2001019710

Puffin Books ISBN 978-0-14-241551-1

Printed in the United States of America

FOR
CARRIE HEATH

AND FOR THE STUDENTS AT
Beginning With Children

Hush, little baby, don't say a word . . .

The mother's dark brown fingers move quickly through a rise of white dough. On the stove, chicken pieces, seasoned and dipped in flour, sizzle. Afternoon sun falls softly over the kitchen. Two girls— one twelve and the other thirteen—are hunched over homework assignments. Dust streams in lines of sun, and the youngest remembers a long time ago when her sister said It's made of bits of skin mostly. I swear. *Skin that's dust, the youngest thinks. Dust that's sun. Sun that's heat that burns the skin. She shakes her head to stop the avalanche of thoughts from coming.*

After a while, she turns in her chair to watch her mother. Watches her knead the dough twice, then pat it down—gently, though, the way she seems to touch everything.

"Are you making biscuits or just plain old bread?" the youngest asks. The mother's hands freeze above the dough. She smiles. She has a pretty smile—her face opens up around it and her dark eyes dance. She is a teacher and her students do all they can to make her smile because it warms them, makes them feel safe even if they're doing division, which many of them haven't yet and may never master. She is brown—all-over brown—hair, eyes, skin. So brown the youngest daughter used to say, "I can eat you like a chocolate bar, Ma," which made the mother laugh. Her mother's brown reminds her of everything she loves: Chocolate. Dark wool. The smell of earth. Trees. The girl and her sister's own skin is coppery—somewhere between their mother's deep brown and their father's lighter skin.

"Biscuits," the mother says. The girls exchange looks and grin. Soon there will be fresh-baked biscuits, fried chicken, a salad of dark leafy greens sprinkled with grated cheese. Coconut cake, left over from

the younger one's birthday—her favorite, and the kind she requests year after year. Soon the father will come home, sit at the head of the table, still dressed in his policeman's uniform, and say, "So, what'd my copper pennies do today?" And the older one will say "Dad!" annoyed that, at thirteen, he is still using this name for both of them. The younger one she can understand—after all, the youngest is still a flat-chested whiny child. But her—she's nearly as tall as he is!

The oldest opens her hand, then closes it again around her pen. Some nights she is afraid her father will never come home. That he will never again walk through that door, take off his hat and his badge, unfasten his holster and place it beside everything else on the table in the mud room. She reads the papers. She knows that cops get killed all the time. Even at her own school she's heard kids say they hate cops. People who don't know her dad's one and people who do, too. The light coming in the kitchen window is yellow-gold, dusty. Years and years of her own family's skin and hair and who knows what. Sometimes she gets so afraid that this will be all that's left of her father. But soon she hears the click of her father's shoes on the porch stairs.

Then he is there, standing tall in the doorway, grinning. "So, what'd my copper pennies do today?" he asks. For the hundredth time. For the thousandth time. For the hundredth thousandth time. And the oldest, Cameron, shakes her head and smiles. The youngest runs to him, jumps up into his arms. Her long legs dangling past his knees.

Later, with the coconut cake still resting in her stomach, the youngest rises from her bed and stares out into the night—the moon is bright yellow, the sky blue-black, the shadows that are the Rocky Mountains. She sniffs, inhaling the scent of pine and cedar and air that is warm still—but with winter at its edges. The beauty of it all stops her breath. When it comes again, her breath is shallow and loud. She has never lived anyplace else and can't imagine it. Doesn't have to because, tonight, this beauty seems to be hers forever.

Her name is Toswiah.

Some mornings, when the sun is bright and the birds are going wild, she wants to hug something, hard—the whole world of it she wants to put her arms around. When she tells her older sister, Cameron looks at her with one eyebrow raised. I have one word for you, Cameron says. Freak.

So she remembers not to tell her sister this—that the world outside her window tonight is perfect. So perfect that sometimes it all seems too much. Too much beauty in one place. All mine, *she whispers, wrapping her arms around herself and laughing.* This world is all mine.

Gone. It is all gone now.

PART ONE

1

THERE IS A SONG THAT GOES *ALL THAT YOU have is your soul*. The singer has this tragic, low voice—like the way someone sounds right after they've been crying for a long time—and she sings the line over and over again until way deep in your heart you believe it's true.

It *is* true.

When it comes down to it, every single other thing can be taken clean away from you. Or you can be taken clean away from it. Like home. More and more and more, Denver feels like a dream I used to have. A place I once belonged to.

When the memory of Denver gets too blurred, I pinch myself and say, *Your name is Toswiah. There was a time when the Rocky Mountains were just outside your window.* But my name isn't Toswiah anymore. And now, this tiny apartment in this crowded city is supposed to be my home. At night, the building echoes with emptiness—the apartments below and above us are empty. When I ask my father how come no one else lives here, he tells me they will come. That eventually someone else will move in, that the Feds thought it'd be best to move us into a building that was empty. I don't believe my father, though. My father is losing his mind. Maybe all of us are.

Yesterday, I saw a girl who looked like a girl I used to know in Denver, and I got so scared and happy all at the same time that my head felt like it was going to lift straight up off my shoulders. As she got closer, I wanted to scream her name. I wanted to say *It's me, Toswiah Green!* Then the girl got closer and I realized it wasn't who I thought it was. She smiled and I smiled back. That was all. Two strangers being nice. She probably didn't even remember it an hour later. But I did.

And hours and hours after that, too, even though I was relieved I didn't know her. Relieved, but sad. Is *sad* the word I'm looking for? No. It's not big enough. What happened inside of me is much stronger than sad. Sad is stupid. It doesn't hurt like this. It doesn't tell even a little bit of the truth—that this *missing* is like someone peeling my skin back each time—peeling it back and exposing everything underneath to air. Hollow? Empty? Frustrated? Lost? Lonely? There're so many words, and none of them work.

Some mornings, waking up in this new place, I don't know where I am. The apartment is tiny. The kitchen is not even a whole room away from the living room, just a few steps and a wide doorway with no door separating it. Not even one fireplace. Daddy sits by the window staring out, hardly ever saying anything. Maybe he thinks if he looks long and hard enough, Denver will reappear, that the cluttered corner store filled with canned stuff, racks and racks of junk food, beer and cigarettes will morph into the hundred-year-old cedar tree at the end of our old street. Maybe he thinks the tall gray buildings all smashed against each other will separate and squat down, that the Rocky Mountains will rise up behind them. I want to say *Daddy, it's never gonna happen.* But I'm afraid he'll break into a million pieces if I do. Become the skin-dust floating around the room. I want to say *Daddy, you did the right thing.*

But I don't know if that's true.

When Daddy looks over to where me and my sister, Anna, sit watching TV, he looks surprised, like he's wondering why we aren't downstairs in the den. No den here, though. No dining room. No extra bathrooms down the hall and at the top of the stairs. Just five rooms with narrow doorways here. Floors covered with linoleum. Walls all painted the same awful shade of blue.

At night, the sounds outside are unfamiliar. Cars honking and people yelling. Fire trucks and ambulances. Anna in bed across the room from me is too close and strange. Every morning, I wake up expecting to see the mountains outside, then sit on the edge of my bed and force the memories to come. I try to push back what is true—that this place is not that place. That we are gone from Denver. Everything about who we were is gone—our names, our pictures, our old clothes and old lives. All that we have is our souls. If a soul is the way you feel deep inside yourself about a thing, the way you love it, the way it stops your breath, then mine is still in Colorado.

Close your eyes and imagine the floor beneath your feet—cool hardwood maybe. Or softly warm and carpeted. Sit down and lift your feet up off of it and imagine you can never put them down on it again. Ever. See how quickly the feeling of that floor fades? See how much you want to feel it again? How lost you feel with no place solid to put your feet?

It's okay to put your feet back down on it. Maybe in your lifetime that floor's not going anywhere.

IMAGINE YOUR BEST FRIEND'S SMILE, HOW YOU remember it from its front-teeth-missing days till this moment. A year after the braces have come off and she's finally learned how to comb that mass of hair. The boys falling over themselves for her. Her name is Lulu.

Toswiah—we have *to get the same outfit. On the first day of school, we'll say we're cousins.*

Imagine Lulu in second grade and third grade and fourth and seventh. The way she shot up past you last year and got beautiful but had her same silly Lulu laugh—even when boys were watching. Lulu in a black turtleneck and jeans—except on the first and last days of school and on our birthday. Then it was something amazing—a long metallic-blue dress made out of silk, shoes with mile-high soles, or a hundred yellow ribbons in her thick black hair and a retro tube top with TONY ORLANDO AND DAWN embroidered across it, halters and miniskirts, a blue leather coat soft as butter falling to her ankles, bright pink lipstick and blue eye shadow. Lulu with her mama's dark skin and her own beautifully slanted eyes, pressing her bleeding finger against mine, whispering *Now our blood's all mixed up. We can't ever leave each other.*

Imagine yourself whispering back *I'm not going anywhere. I'd never leave here in a million years!*

And Lulu laughing, throwing her head back like a grown-up. And Lulu's warm head on my shoulder—the day so perfect, we're speechless.

Lulu. My friend.

My name is Evie. From the jump-rope game. Maybe you've heard the little kids singing *Evie Ivie Over. Here comes a teacher with a big fat stick. I wonder what she's got for arithmetic! One and one? Two! Me and you. Who?*

It came to me as I lay in bed one night—in a half-dream—after me and Lulu had spent the afternoon jumping rope and eating ice-cream sandwiches from a jumbo box of them Lulu's mother had bought, one right after the other until we both swore we'd never eat another one as long as we lived. That night, my father had sat down at the dinner table and told us he was going to testify. *It might mean us leaving here,* he said. *Changing our lives, our names. Everything.* And the ice-cream sandwiches sat heavy in my stomach for a few minutes, then slowly circled around and came back up again.

My name is Evie now. I am tall and skinny and quiet. I've never kissed. Sometimes I think about it, about how it would feel, how it would happen. But maybe it won't ever happen. Not here. Not now. The boys here call me Neckbone, say that's all I am—lots of bone and a little bit of meat. They collect in circles on corners and pass bottles of bright, nasty-looking liquids around. When I walk by them, I feel like a third leg grows out of my butt—my walking gets strange and my body feels all wrong. *Hey Neckbone,* one of them always says, making the others laugh. If I was brave, I would look full at them and say *I'd like a lit-*

tle taste of that. Then I'd take that bottle and put it straight up to my lips, take a long, hard drink of that stuff and wipe my mouth with the back of my hand. If I was brave, I'd slide one of my hands past the waistband of my pants and just stand with it there like they do—holding on to whatever.

If I was brave, I could belong somewhere.

My name's Toswiah, I'd say. *Toswiah Green. Have you ever heard of me?*

But my name is Evie now. And I've never been brave.

When we lived in Denver, we skied and snowboarded. Cameron wasn't afraid. She'd go up to the expert slope and take off. Sometimes I'd stand all bundled up at the bottom of the mountain watching my sister moving toward me. As she got closer, I'd see that she was smiling. Smiling with the snow flying up around her. The sound of her snowboard swishing toward me always made something inside me jump with love and the beauty of it all. Cameron was the brave one. Popular. Smart. *If you try really hard,* she used to say, *maybe a little of me will rub off on you.* And although I stuck my tongue out at her when she said this, I did try because I wanted to know what it felt like to come down that mountain—grinning and beautiful and free.

Hey Neckbone, one of those guys always says. *Show a brother some love.*

I CAN NEVER TELL ANYBODY THE REAL TRUTH. But I can write it and say this story you're about to read is *fiction.* I can give it a beginning, middle and end. A plot. A character named Evie. A sister named Anna.

Call it fiction because fiction's what it is. Evie and Anna aren't real people. So you can't go somewhere and look this up and say *Now I know who this story's about.*

Because if you did, it would kill my father.

Summer. Mama's making pork chops and singing at the top of her lungs. She sings the words over and over: "We come from the mountains, we come from the mountains. Let's go back to the mountains and turn the world around." It's Cameron's tenth birthday, so Mama just laughs when Cameron stands up on a chair and says, "I am in my two-digit numbers now!" Cameron's hair is wild around her head. One of her side teeth looks like a fang, and the two front ones stick out past her lips. Mama and Daddy are threatening braces. When Cameron hears them talking about it, she closes her mouth tight and runs. Outside, the sun has gone down but the kitchen is still hot. Mama looks out the window and her eyebrows knit up, but she keeps on singing even though it's already late and Daddy's not home. Sometimes she says "I wish I wasn't married to a cop!" She smiles when she says it, though—like maybe she's both sorry and proud.

And later, Cameron with her braces on, sneaking looks in the mirror when she thinks no one is watching—at eleven, twelve, and then thirteen, and the braces pliered off, her teeth cleaned, her lips spreading across her face to grin every time she could think to. And in the evening, back in the mirror, whispering to herself, "I am beautiful."

Mama in the kitchen, older now, too, but still glancing out the window on the nights when Daddy's late getting home.

2

WE LEFT DENVER IN THE MIDDLE OF THE NIGHT with some clothes and some family pictures, toothbrushes and combs, all in plastic bags since our suitcases were monogrammed. The morning before we left, two Jehovah's Witnesses rang our bell. Mama answered the door but unlike the other times Jehovah's Witnesses came by our house, she didn't say "No, thank you" and close it again. She bought a *Watchtower*, an *Awake!* and a small brown book called *Reasoning the Scriptures*.

But you don't have a religious bone in your body, my sister said to her.

What do I have? Mama asked. Then she shook her head, brushed the hair back from Cameron's forehead and tried to smile. *You know I don't mean that.* But she packed the literature into her bag.

This morning, I tried to remember my grandmother's face. I tried to remember the evening she came by to say she couldn't come with us, that Denver was the place she'd always known and she couldn't see herself at seventy-five going to start a new life somewhere.

"Look at these hands," she said, holding out her hands to show us the way the veins pushed up against her dark skin. "These hands belong to an old lady. At night, my teeth go in a glass and the arthritis feels like it wants to get the best of me. Denver's the only place I've ever lived. And I never planned on not dying here."

Mama's eyes started tearing, but Grandma put a finger to her lips. "Hush now," Grandma said. "Don't start that. You'll see me again," she said. "You will."

The afternoon before the men came, we kissed my

grandmother good-bye as she sat rocking slowly in her blue chair. I've never seen my grandmother cry, but that day, her chin quivered just the tiniest bit before she sniffed and said *This isn't how I want you all to remember me.*

I stood a little bit away from all of them—Mama, Daddy and Cameron—remembering how Grandma used to say *This rocker will belong to you one day, Toswiah.* I watched everyone doing what they could not to cry, thinking *That day's never gonna come.* Even then, though, it wasn't a hundred percent real to me. As I stood there in the middle of my grandma's living room with the Denver sun coming in through the thin yellow curtains, I thought *This is all just a game, a stupid game. Tomorrow Daddy will say, "I changed my mind. This is all too much to leave behind."*

But what I know now is this: Look at your grandmother's face. Remember the lines. Touch her cheekbones. Hold the memory of her in your fingers, in your eyes, in your mind. It might be all you get to keep.

Left behind is that rocker and one Toswiah Green, standing with her arms folded, on a tree-lined street in

Colorado. If one of my old classmates shows a group picture around, someone might ask *Who's that?* And the classmate will answer *That was Toswiah. She just disappeared one day. Weird, huh?*

MAMA SAYS THE LIES WE'RE FORCED TO TELL are God's will. She believes God sent His Witnesses to our door that morning for a reason. *He knew I'd need them,* she says.

Mama's wrapped her arms around God's legs, Anna says. *I guess she figures He'll drag her to a better place.*

These days, Mama prays and prays. *One day the end is going to come,* she says.

I don't tell her it came a long time ago.

PUT YOUR FEET DOWN ON MY OLD FLOORS IN Denver and keep walking. See the pictures of the four of us—Mama, Daddy, me and Cameron, smiling. *Those are cool names,* you say. *Cameron and Toswiah.* If you want, you can have them. They don't belong to us anymore. Take the gray-carpeted stairs two at a time, the way me and my sister used to do. See the spot at the top of the stair that's flattened? Matt Cat used to sleep there because the sun came through the skylight and shined right on him. Listen. Can you hear him purring? Go to the right and you're in my room. Pretty. Plain. The room smells of pencil shavings. The stack of journals that I've kept since I was old enough to write haven't yet been destroyed. Open the top one to the last page:

They don't know I hear them talking late at night when they think me and Cameron are asleep. Daddy says Mr. Dennis and Mr. Randall killed that boy. He wants to be a witness to it—break the Blue Wall of Silence. That's what he calls it. I never thought of silence that way—blue. A whole wall of it. Like a swimming pool gone wrong. Like blue gelato ices that me and Lulu scrape with wooden spoons. Eat till our lips and tongues are dark blue-black as aliens'. Or dead people's.

The letters and birthday cards, monogrammed towels and the toys we played with when we were little kids. The green sweater with TOSSY knitted into it in yellow letters, the TOSSY T baseball cap I used to wear backward. TGIF—TOSWIAH GREEN IS FABULOUS on a pillowcase—a gift from Lulu for my twelfth birthday. Gone. Gone. Gone. Keep walking. Down the long carpeted hall into Cameron's girlie, pink room with its frilled white curtains and huge GIRL POWER poster on the ceiling. In the corner of the left window, you'll find a heart painted bright red with a black Magic-Markered arrow through it and the letters C & J. Joseph—the boy she used to love.

These are the things we left behind.

When they sell our house, the new people will ask, "Who lived here before?" and the Realtor will give them someone else's name. She will say, "It was a nice single man, I hear." Or maybe she'll say, "A young couple, I think—no kids of their own, but lots of nieces and nephews often coming to visit." They won't ask why that bedroom at the end of the hall is painted pink and still smells of Cameron's Love's Baby Soft perfume. The journals on my desk will be long gone, so the wife won't pick one up and flip through it. Won't say to her husband, "Honey, listen to this . . ."

My name is Evie now, and here is Evie's story. She grew up in San Francisco—Pine off of Divisadero. Kind of the border between Pacific Heights and Western Addition. Yeah, of course she knows where Golden Gate Park is. She used to go there all the time. Did you ever see the two-headed snake at the Exploratorium? Did you ever go to the Pork Store Restaurant? Yeah, Evie loved shopping in the Haight, too. They have the coolest clothes over there! But you know what she really misses? Ghirardelli's at the Wharf. And good sourdough bread and clam chowder. Don't you?

3

It is Saturday. Rainy. My father sits by the window, squinting down at something. I know there is nothing there. He is whispering the Miranda rights—*You have the right to remain silent. Anything you say can be held against you in a court of law. You have the right to an attorney*—over and over again until maybe he believes it now. I sit on the couch watching him secretly, my book open on my lap. When I look back down at the book, the words are spilling over the page and off. The story is about a little girl who finds a dog. The girl in the story is white. The dog isn't. They love each other instantly, and when she brings him home, her parents smile and say *Of course you can keep it.*

There weren't a whole lot of other blacks in Denver. Cops were our family. Cops were our friends. Daddy was the only black one in his precinct. It was different there, though. Black. White. It didn't matter. Cops were cops. We were all one big family. All on the same side of the law. We were the good guys. For years and years that was true.

My father lifts up his arms and lets them fall. He gets quiet again. There is nothing in his eyes anymore. Anna sees it and turns away. Mama sees it and opens her Bible. There isn't any other place for me to look. In the novel the girl and her family and her dog will live happily ever after. Even though I know what the ending's gonna be, I keep reading.

The rain slams against the window. The panes rattle. The gray here isn't like anything I've ever imagined. It is heavy and thick and feels like it's never going to go away. I turn the page of the book and stare down at the floating words. The tears hurt when they

finally come, spilling down onto the pages. I am not
the girl. I am not the dog. Who am I?

Who

Am

I?

Daddy's patrol car pulls up beside us. Cameron has her cheerleading uniform on under her coat. She is shivering. It is dark. The air smells like snow. We climb into the back, and Daddy turns the heat on full blast. When I press my hand against the metal grate separating us from Daddy, I shiver and try to imagine what it's like to be under arrest. Daddy drives slowly. I press my head against the glass until my face feels like it's going to freeze. At school today, our teacher asked us who we were. She said, "Describe yourself to someone who's just meeting you." When my turn came, I stood up and said, "My name is Toswiah Green. My favorite color is blue. I am tall for my age. My best friend is Lulu. These are the facts," I said. "The facts speak for themselves." The class laughed. Some even clapped and cheered. When I sat down again, I felt my whole body get warm. "I am Toswiah Green," I whispered. "That's a fact!"

Daddy's car moves slowly through our neighborhood. Some people smile and wave. Little kids run along the curb, yelling "Hi, Policeman!" and waving crazily.

Cameron chants her cheers softly—"We are the mighty, mighty Tigers. You can't beat the mighty, mighty Tigers. . . ."

4

IN FIFTH GRADE OUR TEACHER ASKED US TO write about the most wonderful thing we'd ever seen. I sat in class tapping my pencil against my head trying to remember the colors of butterflies' wings and how the deep blue-green water of Glenwood Springs made you think of something that went on forever. But none of the things that came to my mind was the prettiest. When I started writing, it was about my father, the year he won the police department's Medal for Bravery for rescuing a mother and her baby son from a man who was holding them hostage. He'd been a cop all of my life, and I had never really thought much about what he did or what it meant. On the morning of the ceremony, my father wore his other uniform— a dark jacket with a leather belt, brass buttons and gold epaulets at the shoulders. When he walked into the living room, my sister and I stopped fighting over the TV remote and stared at him. We had never seen him dressed this way, and he looked like the tallest, proudest, most beautiful man that ever lived.

Why are you copper pennies sitting there with your mouths open? he said, laughing. *You act like you've never seen me before in your life.*

And we hadn't—not like that. Not standing there looking like someone who would protect us from the world ending. Someone who could, if he had to, push us behind him then stop an oncoming bullet with his hand.

Daddy . . . , my sister said, *you look awesome.*

That morning, as I sat there between Cameron and Mama in the audience listening to the lieutenant go on about my father's bravery, I felt like I was someone special. Like all of us were special.

THINGS FALL APART. I KNOW THIS NOW. Sometimes it happens fast—like the time my sister came down wrong on her ankle and missed a whole season of cheerleading. What I remember is her sitting in her room every night, crying. Or the time my mother cut her finger with a steak knife. While my father rushed her to the hospital, Cameron and I were left to finish dinner, get it on the table and sit there for two hours, staring at our food. Scared that Mama would come back one finger short of the hand she had left with.

But sometimes things fall apart slowly. When the lieutenant pinned that medal to my father's chest, it was the beginning of the Greens ending. Months later, my father would say *When I saw you all sitting in that front row cheering me on, some little seed started to grow in my brain.* He said it was a seed of faith in his family and the Denver Police Department. A seed that made him believe in the possibility of perfection . . . and trust . . . and loyalty. As my father looked out at us from the stage while reporters flashed pictures and other cops shook his hand, he smiled and winked at me. I winked back, not knowing that what was growing in his mind was a seed of justice that

33

would one day lead to the biggest decision he'd ever have to make in his life.

Mama raised her hand to her lips and blew Dad a kiss. Then we were being called up to the stage, all of us, hugging Daddy and smiling for the press. *Perfect*, one reporter said. *Absolutely perfect.*

And for years, I believed we were.

The night after the shooting, I came downstairs to find my father sitting on the couch staring into the darkness. I sat beside him and we talked quietly— about school and friends and Cameron and Mama. We talked around the shooting until he made me go back to bed. After that, I came downstairs every night, after Mama and Cameron had gone to bed. Maybe it was because I insisted on sitting awhile in the dark with him night after night. Maybe it was because I was his baby daughter, the one who'd still be there after my big sister was gone. Or maybe it was just because he needed someone to talk to. For whatever reason, my father began to reveal what happened in bits and pieces. What I learned in those late-night talks was that my father had witnessed a murder. A fifteen-year-old boy had been killed by two cops who were close to our family. My father wouldn't tell me their names at first, but he said over and over, *Something's got to be done, Toswiah. It isn't justice. It isn't right.*

I knew something had to be done, but more than that I knew if the cops were in my daddy's precinct, they'd been at one of my birthday parties, had given me a lift home from school, had pulled my braid at some point in my life and handed me a toy or book or lollipop. I'd grown up with the cops in Denver and couldn't imagine any of them shooting a boy. Again and again I saw the ghost-boy falling but couldn't see the face of the cop who held the gun. Again and again I tried to think of which cop it could be until the hand holding the gun followed me into my dreams, to school, even to the bathroom in the middle of the night.

The boy was an honor student, the only child of a high school English teacher. A single mom. The boy was only in tenth grade but was already getting mail from colleges. My father knew all this from newspaper reports he'd read and research he'd done. Even though the cops had said they thought the boy reached for a gun, my father knew it wasn't true. As my father talked about the boy, he became more real. I didn't know his name, but I felt like I didn't have to. He was black and I was black, and maybe somewhere along the way we would've met. Maybe we would've become friends. I imagined the boy holding a basketball above his head, saying *Like this, Toswiah. Just let it roll off your fingers and fly.* I imagined us riding bikes around the neighborhood, stopping to buy ice-cream cones doubledipped in rainbow sprinkles. When he smiled, his whole face melted into something soft and amazing. People waved and smiled back. People called out to us. I imagined his mother walking into his empty room and calling his name, standing there all night long waiting for him to answer.

My father said *What would you do, T?*

I shrugged, and stared down at my hands. *What's the right thing, Daddy?*

Exactly, he said, frowning into the darkness. He sighed and kissed my head. *Both choices seem so damn wrong.*

Then he sent me off to bed.

I lay in bed and stared up at the ceiling all night. I thought about my father—how the love I felt for him some days made my throat hollow out. I thought about his smile, the way it always came, shy and slow, and the way his eyes lit up when me and my sister appeared suddenly, riding our bikes alongside his patrol car. I thought about the way he used to braid my hair on Sundays, how his hands felt soft and sure. Wherever he went, I'd go. I couldn't imagine a world, a life, a day without him.

I closed my eyes then, trying to imagine what it felt like to watch someone die, someone innocent and scared. Pictures flashed in and out of my brain—that boy crying out then falling; my father running to him; the other cops standing there, their hands dumbly hanging at their sides. The echo of the gunshots. Everyone's surprise.

Outside my window, the moon hung down low, close to the mountains. Every now and then, a cloud moved past it.

Cops murdering. Cops murdering a black kid. White cops murdering a black kid. My father turning at the first shot to see the kid standing there, his arms raised above his head. The second and third shots. The kid falling. My father's face, first surprise, then anger, then fear maybe—that his friends could do this, could be so afraid of a black boy that they could shoot without thinking, without remembering that he, Officer Green, was black, that black wasn't a dangerous thing.

"No . . . ," my father said softly, the way he says it now when he sits alone at the window. "God, please, no. . . ."

Outside my window, the night got darker, then slowly faded to gray.

OFFICER RANDALL, MY FATHER SAID SLOWLY when I asked him for the fifth time who the cops were. *Randall and Dennis, Toswiah. That's who killed the boy.*

As he said their names, the floor began to slide out from beneath me. Mr. Randall and Mr. Dennis. Men I had known my whole life. Officer Dennis, who always had a silly joke to tell *(Hey Toswiah, what do you get when you cross a skunk and peanut butter? Something very smelly sticking to the roof of your mouth!)* and Officer Randall, who was tall and gray-eyed and had a son named Joseph, who Cameron was in love with.

"He came out of nowhere," Officer Randall had said, his hands shaking, his face crumbling with the horror of what he'd just done. After a moment, he added, "He startled us, Green."

Officer Dennis was there, turning toward my father, easing his gun back into the holster, his voice unsure. "We thought he had a gun. He was going for something." Then cursing, his bottom lip starting to quiver with the weight of it all.

"He was facing you," my father said. "He was just standing there with his hands up."

Then Officer Dennis's voice drops just the tiniest bit. His eyes narrow. I swallow. I've known Officer Dennis all my life, but in this moment, I don't know him at all.

"We thought he had a gun!"

5

THE PHONE CALLS STARTED COMING A DAY
after the shooting.

If Green says a word, a raspy voice said, *we'll kill
him.* I held the phone away from my ear, then closer
again, pressing it hard against my head. The voice went
away then. A minute later, there was a dial tone. Then
the loud beep and another voice telling me that the
phone was off the hook. I couldn't hang up though. Even
though the beep pounded into my ear and my hand hurt
from holding the phone too tight, I couldn't hang up.

When Mama came into the living room a little

while later, she found me standing there, my face twisted up in horror, tears streaming down my nose and into my mouth.

The second time the raspy voice called, my mother snatched the phone out of the wall and screamed. I was sitting at the kitchen table eating a jelly sandwich.

Cameron was at cheerleading practice. When she came home that night, she threw her blue and gold pom-poms on the floor and said *Everyone at school is acting so weird. I hate my stupid life!*

Joseph had started it. After the shooting, he began spreading the word around school that our father was a liar. That he was trying to ruin Joseph's life. Joseph was tall like his father, gray-eyed, too. He played guard on the basketball team and was a running back on the football team. Girls followed him and giggled. Boys held up their hands, feeling important when he slapped them five. Cameron had gone to the movies with him, had let him walk her home, had kissed him beneath the bleachers at the football field. She said the first time he took her hand, his was so sweaty, she wanted to laugh out loud. Said *Maybe that's when I started falling in love.*

And when Joseph chose Cameron, the other cheerleaders, who she knew had always called her *The Only* behind her back, frowned. One even asked, "But why *you?*"

I wanted to slap her, Cameron told me. *I wanted to die.* Then softer, she said *Sometimes I hate being black. Don't you?*

And I didn't answer. Because, back then, I couldn't imagine being anything else. I loved Mama's skin, loved the way it smelled and felt. I loved looking in the mirror and seeing my own brown face staring back at me. Even if there weren't a whole lot of black people in Denver, the mayor was black and I was black and Lulu was, too. And my family and Grandma. The thought of waking up anything or anybody else scared me.

I thought white people weren't mean to black people about race stuff. I thought Denver wasn't that kind of place. But the morning Joseph walked into the school and said my father was a liar, only a few kids doubted him. Only a few kids, who had heard their own parents saying *White cops, black kid dead,* turned away. When the paper ran a story about Raymond Taylor, only a few kids thought to themselves *It could've been me.*

There's this thing called the Blue Wall of Silence in

the police world. It means all cops are brothers and sisters and should never betray one another. You swear to it in your heart when you become a cop. It's not written anywhere, you just know it. You know that cops are there for you no matter what. My father told me you believe hard in it because you have to. You have to be able to trust your fellow cop. No matter what. There had always been cops in my life—hanging at our barbecues and parties, coming to my class to speak about crime, taking me and Cameron along with their kids to trick-or-treat, bringing over armfuls of Christmas presents. There were undercover cops, too—who, if we begged enough, lifted their pants' legs to show us the guns concealed there, or made us squeal by telling us cops-and-robbers stories where the bad guy almost got away but was caught at the last minute because of one daredevil feat or another. There were beat cops walking our neighborhood, calling us by name, and traffic cops coming up to our car to say hello.

SIX DAYS AFTER THE SHOOTING, INSPECTOR Albert Oliver showed up at our house just before we sat down to dinner. When Mama asked him to join us, he shook his head and said he needed to talk to Daddy outside. Inspector Oliver was tall and white-haired, even though he wasn't old. I didn't know him as well as I knew other cops, but I liked what I knew of him. He was always shy and polite around Mama, Cameron and me, speaking softly and taking each of our hands in both of his to say hello.

It was a Monday night in April. Denver was just starting to get warm. Mama had opened the French doors leading from the kitchen to the back deck, but the air coming in was still more cold than warm. When Cameron got up to close the door, Mama gave her a fierce look and shook her head. Cameron frowned and sat down again. My father stood on our deck in his police uniform. He had taken his holster off and laid it on a chair. Without it, he looked smaller. He put his hands on the porch railing and sighed.

We sat around the kitchen table, each of us leaning toward the door to listen. I could just barely hear Inspector Oliver's voice.

"Think hard, Green. Randall and Dennis might be the wrong people to go after. I'm not saying they didn't do it—I'm not saying they did, either," he said slowly. "It's just that cophood's all those men have. Who knows what they'll do?"

I stared at my plate, feeling sick. Mama had made lasagna with spinach and roasted red peppers. Beside my piece of lasagna, there was salad. Any other time, it would have been one of my favorite meals. But that night, my stomach was turning over and over again. When had Randall, with his silly laugh, and Dennis, whose face broke into the biggest grin when he saw me and Cameron, become the wrong people? They were our friends.

"I know what I'm doing," my father said, his voice shaking. "That boy getting killed was wrong. You *know* it, Al. I can't let them go back to work knowing what I know."

He got quiet for a minute.

"What about next time?" my father said. "What about Raymond Taylor's family?"

"They thought it was gang related—"

"Because he was black. That boy was standing, facing them, with his hands raised. And they shot him. Both of them. Bullets came from *both* guns. We both know that. We *all* know that."

Inspector Oliver didn't say anything. Maybe he was staring at my father like he was seeing him for the first time, like he was just realizing my father was the same color as Raymond Taylor. And the same color as the mayor of Denver.

After a moment he said, "Officer Dennis said he was reaching for—"

"He wasn't reaching for *anything*, Albert. *Anything*. He was shot standing! I saw it."

"You guys've been friends for a long time. You three—"

"Officer Randall had called for backup because he thought it was gang related, thought it was a lot more than one. When I pulled up, that *boy*—he was a *boy*—came out from behind those cars with his hands raised and stopped. He was *stopped*." My father's voice broke.

I got up suddenly and walked quickly to the door. Behind me, Mama called my name, but I ignored her. I hated the sound in my father's voice. *Hated* it.

I moved across the deck to the patio swing. Both Daddy and Inspector Oliver were staring out into the darkness. My father turned then, looked at me like he was starting to tell me to go inside. But he didn't.

"He was standing, Albert. He was standing and now he's dead."

Wind blew, rustling the plastic covering the barbecue grill. Otherwise, it was stone-cold quiet.

The inspector fussed with a cuticle while he spoke. "Officer Dennis and Officer Randall've been cops for a long time. Their daddies were cops, and their daddies' daddies. Something must have scared them bad to just shoot—"

"And what about the things that scare *me*? I'm sick of this. Gang talk and everybody looks my way." Daddy looked hard at Inspector Oliver. "Anyone stop to think that there aren't even enough black boys in Denver to make up an all-black gang?"

When Inspector Oliver didn't say anything, Daddy went on.

"He was *standing*, Al. He was standing and he was black. And you know and I know and everyone on the force knows those gangs everyone is so afraid of are not made up of black boys."

"You'd be taking their dreams away, Green. The only thing these men have."

I folded my arms across my chest and shivered. The raspy voice came into my head again. Felt like it had grown hands and wrapped them around my throat. I looked at Daddy and swallowed hard.

"What about the only thing *I* have? You think I know how to be anything else but a cop? A cop who's a father, that's all that I am." He pressed his fingers to his eyes and sighed. "I know how to protect, Al. You know why?"

Inspector Oliver raised his eyebrows slightly, like he knew Daddy would go on whether he said anything or not.

"Because I've got two daughters. Two. You think I brought them into this world to turn around and watch them get killed for no reason at all? That could have been Toswiah with a hat on standing there. They could have seen her and saw something threatening." Daddy raised his voice then quickly lowered it again. "That could have been *my* girl. It could have been my wife at the other end of that phone line being told her daughter had been shot!"

I stared down at my hands, trying to imagine Mama getting a call that I'd been killed. I saw my own house collapsing in on itself, the roof and walls crumbling.

"What makes you think the D.A.'s going to believe you?" Inspector Oliver said.

My father looked at him but didn't say anything. Matt Cat pushed the screen door open and jumped into my lap. He circled once then lay across it.

"I'm playing devil's advocate here. You're making it about race, so I'm—"

"I'm not making it." My father shook his head. I could feel his exasperation across the deck. "It *is* about race. If Raymond Taylor was white, I don't think he'd be dead now."

Inspector Oliver shrugged. "We don't know that, and we'll probably never know that. What I'm saying is, two white cops against a black cop," he said slowly, counting off on his fingers. He raised his other hand. "A black kid dead."

After a moment, Daddy turned and looked over at me again. Something caught in his eyes. We stared at each other without saying anything for a long time, then Daddy shook his head and turned back to the inspector.

"I believe in the law, Albert," Daddy said quietly. "I wouldn't be a cop if I didn't. My father was a lawyer and his father was a judge. And here I am—a cop. You say it's in Randall's and Dennis's blood—well, it's in mine, too. They shouldn't have killed Taylor. I'm going to stand by that." He looked out into the darkness. When he started talking again, his voice was low and scratchy. "I'm going to stand by that no matter what, because the way I see it, the way I've taught my girls to see it—blood's the same color no matter who it's flowing through."

You can pause a video, rewind it, press stop and power and make it disappear. Right there, that evening with Inspector Albert Oliver standing on our porch biting on his cuticle, is the point where I'd pause. Then I'd press stop and my father would still be a cop in Denver, his uniform pressed, his shoes shined, his face calm and smiling.

6

THERE WEREN'T MANY BLACK PEOPLE IN DEN-
ver, but the ones who lived there were angry. There was
a protest. And a rally. There was a small riot in down-
town Denver. Two black ministers gave sermons about
injustice that made the local paper. We weren't churchgoing and we didn't march. But the rage was in the air
all around us. And in the center of it, there was Daddy,
the only black cop in his precinct, coming home from
work after a day with not a single white cop speaking to
him. The white cops who had been our friends became
strangers. Me and Cameron walked from the bus stop

and no cop car slowed down to ask if we were Green's copper pennies. The white cops made believe they didn't know us; the black ones from other precincts acknowledged my father but stayed clear of him. At night, my father would sit at the dining room table and tell us of the phone calls he'd gotten—anonymous calls from men who identified themselves as cops. "You're doing the right thing, Green," they'd whisper

"They know what I know," my father said softly, staring down at his plate without touching his food. "All my life I've walked into the precinct as a black cop. But I was a cop first, so when the racist jokes were flying, I let them slap me on the back and sometimes laughed right along with them—even had my own to tell about white folks. It was like that—black, white, we were all cops, that's all. Cops first." He balled his hand into a fist and stared at it. Then stared at me, his eyes starting to water. I swallowed, hating Randall and Dennis and every cop that had brought us to this moment. "Cops first. That's always been the rule. No matter what. When I saw that boy falling, I wasn't a cop anymore."

Seven days after the shooting, the mayor called for a full investigation. A few days after that, Daddy met with the district attorney.

We can protect you, the D.A. said. *But it might mean having to leave here. Ask yourself if it's worth it.*

That night at dinner, Daddy said *I'm a man, I can testify.* He walked slowly through every room of the house, touching the walls, picking up pictures and putting them down again, fluffing pillows and pressing them to his face. When he got back to the kitchen, he sat down at the table and said *We can leave here.* Then he leaned into his fists and cried.

Two days after my father met with the district attorney, he sat me and Cameron down at the kitchen table to tell us we'd be leaving. By then, I had known this was coming. I had been listening to him and Mama go back and forth about the consequences. The night before, I had walked in on Mama sitting at the kitchen table, marking spelling exams and crying. But Cameron had gone on like nothing was happening, even though every radio station in Colorado was telling the story.

"I can't believe you're gonna screw up our lives like this," Cameron yelled.

"I'd want someone to do this if it was one of you," my father said.

"They didn't kill *us*," Cameron said. "Don't do this to *us*, Daddy."

At dusk, someone fired three shots through our kitchen window. I was upstairs in my room, spying on my father. I could see him from my window, standing on the back deck, staring out at the trees, every now and then his shoulders rising and falling. Cameron was in the basement. Mama had just walked out of the kitchen to set the table for dinner.

Outside, a few birds were making noise. When I ran downstairs, Mama was slumped against the dining room wall, her head in her hands. Daddy was beside her, his arms around her shoulders. Cameron stood in the corner of the dining room, hugging herself hard. Glass covered the kitchen table and floor. The bullet holes were like small black caves against the white kitchen wall. I stared at them without blinking. I was not afraid. Some part of us that had been the same way forever was gone. The holes in the walls proved it. The dead boy, his mother in his room at night calling and calling his name. I thought of dead people in the movies. How their eyes flutter open like magazines. I thought *This part of my life is over now.*

7

MAYBE SOMEWHERE IN HIS HEAD MY FATHER
imagined Raymond Taylor as his own son. Maybe he
looked at us in that moment and saw two daughters—
his copper pennies—safe, but not safe. Girls. But black
girls. And me, tall and skinny and always running and
climbing trees and, even at thirteen, still coming home
with skinned knees and jammed fingers. Me, who was
always begging to have my braid chopped off so I
didn't have to deal with my hair every day, closer to a
boy in some ways than a girl. Maybe he looked at me,

his youngest copper penny, and thought *It could happen like this.*

Me and Cameron sat there, my love for Daddy blossoming into something deeper, Cameron's disgust growing fast as a weed.

Later that night, I walked into the den to find him holding a picture of himself with the cops in his precinct.

"I don't feel safe anymore," he said. He put down the picture and left the room.

I looked at the picture for a long time after he left. I had known everyone in that picture my whole life. Twenty-two officers, all in blue. Look again, though. Blue and white. Blue and white. Blue and white. Then Daddy. Blue and black. Look again. Harder. Longer.

That night, the men came for us.

8

MY MOTHER USED TO LISTEN TO HER OLD records all the time. She'd put the album on our old turntable and set the needle down gently. Then the music would lift up around the room. Sad, cloudy-sounding music. Songs about people going off to look for America and hearts being broken. Songs where the men sounded like they were singing with the last breaths they had in the world and the women sang low and gravelly about men coming and going. Now the songs come to me—bits of phrases, pieces of tunes. They come to me late at night when I'm not expecting them. Words and words and words. *You know us,* they whisper. *You know us.*

When the men came, the moon was out, hanging down close outside my window. I'd never seen it that way before—full and yellow and looking close enough to touch. The men came in the night with guns under their coats and the moon saying its own good-bye. Their coming surprised me. And then it didn't. They'd always been coming. From the day I was born they'd been coming. Lulu used to say that we're just paper dolls made at one of God's play dates. *He knows the scene,* she'd say. *From start to finish already. Even if we don't have a clue.* When the men came, something stepped outside of me and watched with its arms folded. Nodding. As the men drove us away, that something lifted its hand and waved. I watched it. I *was* it. It's gone now.

Lulu lived five doors down from us. Earlier that evening, before the bullets came through the kitchen window, she had tiptoed up to my room and hugged me the way she had done so many nights before.

We had known we would be leaving but didn't know exactly when. Each morning before school, Lulu and I hugged each other hard—thankful for another day together. Each night, we cried and said our good-byes. Lulu and I had been born in the same hospital. Our mothers said we turned toward each other in our neighboring incubators and smiled. We were both born a month too soon in the middle of the night. We both weighed less than five pounds. When Lulu left my room, I pressed my face against the pane and cried.

Cameron was in her own room. Months later, she would tell me that when the men came, she was in the middle of writing a letter to Joseph. *I think I loved him once,* she said. *I hope you don't ever have to know what it's like to leave a guy you loved.*

I loved Lulu, I said. *And Grandma. And Matt Cat.*

It's different, though. The way I felt for Joseph, before he started saying all that stupid stuff and showing his true colors, is . . . I don't know. It's something in your heart. You don't get it. You're too young.

I'm old enough to know we only have one heart, I said. *Love is love.*

THE MEN WERE QUIET, TALL. ONE BLACK. ONE white. When Cameron asked where the next place was, the men said it was too unsafe to tell us. We climbed into a van with blacked-out windows. Matt Cat had gone to live with Grandma two days before. But as the van rumbled off, I swore I could hear him howling.

The black man wore a yellow jacket. The white one wore a peacoat. The black one's hair was cut like my father's—a little on the top, the sides and back shaved close. He was the one who told us what our last name would be.

You'll have to pick new first ones, he said.

Toswiah was my grandmother's name and her mother's name, too. Whenever I told someone my name for the first time, I had to spell it out for them. *Toswiah,* I'd say slowly—pronouncing it *Tos-wee-ah* so that it didn't get mispronounced. Then I'd wait for them to go on about how unusual it was. I am tall and narrow like Cameron and Mama. We wear our hair the same way—pulled back into a braid that stops between our shoulders. Our hair is kinky enough to stay braided without any elastics or barrettes. We all three have the same square jaw and sharp cheekbones. *Striking,* my mother used to say. *Does that mean pretty?* I'd ask her. But she'd just smile and shake her head, tell me being pretty didn't matter. Cameron has eyebrows like our father—thick and black. Sometimes I think she's beautiful. Sometimes I can't stand the sight of her. The night we left Denver, we were dressed almost alike—blue hooded sweatshirts underneath purple down vests. Cameron was wearing the tights and turtleneck from her cheerleading outfit and a long black skirt. I was wearing jeans.

Are you twins, the black one asked.

Of course not, Cameron said. *Jeez!*

Toswiah and Cameron—Jonathan and Shirley Green's girls. My name is Evie now. *Evil Evie. Evie Ivie Over. Here comes a teacher with a big fat stick. . . .* For more than thirteen years I'd been Toswiah. Then came an end to that system of things.

First they took our names away.

Then the house would be sold, the money from it tunneled through this system and that system until it became a check for Evan Thomas. We were running away from death in a black minivan with a brown leather interior. It wasn't our car, the old brown BMW. That car was behind us, too. As we drove away, I closed my eyes, trying to remember Lulu and that yellow moon. The night got quieter. I knew Denver was growing smaller and smaller behind me.

It was late May. The air smelled like pine and cedar. I took a deep breath and tried to hold it. Tried to hold on. Cameron pulled her vest over her head and cried. Our mother sat with her hands in her lap. Daddy stared at the blacked-out window. His face was blank as the pane.

When I closed my eyes, I wasn't in the van anymore. I was back at our house, waving good-bye to these strangers. Holding my father's hand.

9

AFTER WE LEFT DENVER, DAYS GOT ALL WEIRD. We'd wake up and it would be Thursday and I couldn't remember the weekend before. For the three months in between this apartment and Denver we stayed in a place called a safe house. It was an old motel, falling apart and empty save for us and the men who'd driven us out of Denver. Each morning, Mama would give them a grocery list and one of them would leave, returning hours later with bags of food and supplies. Sometimes Daddy had to go with them and testify. When he left, minutes passed slowly and the hours went on and on. When Daddy returned, the sun was usually down. He'd look tired. On those evenings, he went into his bedroom without saying anything and wouldn't come out again till late the next afternoon. No one would tell us where we were, and after a while we stopped asking. I knew we were still in Colorado, because I could see the mountains. But there were no houses nearby and no major roads. The television got only three channels. One night as I was flipping among them, I saw my father's face on the screen. *Turn it off,* my mother said quickly. After that, we were only allowed to watch the videos the men brought back for us. Before they gave them to us, they took them out of their plastic rental cases so we wouldn't even know the name of the video store.

"I feel like I'm going crazy," Cameron said. "I feel like I'm going to *die.*"

I didn't tell her, but I felt like we had already died. We were nowhere. We were nothing. Two grown-ups and two kids waiting to be reborn. Cameron cried and screamed outright, but I cried late at night, in the darkness, holding the sobs in so hard, it felt like my chest was going to explode.

I wanted to be brave.

Three months—of not seeing anybody but each other and the men who were working on the case until me and Cameron thought we were going to rip each other's necks off or die trying.

"I think I'm from another family," Cameron said one night. Our beds were about three feet apart. The room was tiny and smelled of old carpeting and rust. I stared at Cameron's profile. The moon was coming in through the window, and the little bit of light from it made her look about a hundred years old.

"I think I was switched at birth and separated from my real parents," she said. "They're sane and living somewhere in Colorado. They have some other children, including your real sister, who they took home by mistake, instead of me. She's a lot more like you than I am. They go on picnics. My real mother's into line dancing. It embarrasses my real sister and brother, just like it would embarrass me. Your real sister doesn't care, though. It makes my mother happy."

Cameron sighed, then turned toward the window. "The name she gave your real sister is supposed to be my name. Your sister still has it. Nothing in her life has changed. She's happy and well-adjusted." I could hear her crying softly. "I can't believe this is happening to me."

"It's not forever," I said.

She sniffed. "Not this skanky place. But everything else is. Everything."

I turned onto my back and stared up at the ceiling. Lulu was back in that real world. I stuck my arm into the air. In the weird moonlight, it looked dark blue and skinny enough to be out of some creep show. I reached my hand up higher, stretching it until my shoulder and back hurt. If I stretched it back in time, back around Lulu's shoulder, it would get cut right off. Someone would find it back in Denver, recognize it as part of the Green family and trace it right to us here, where nobody's supposed to know where we are.

"I'm going back someday."

"You can't," Cameron said. "You know that."

"Someday," I said again. "I don't believe in forever. That's too long a time."

I didn't tell her that Lulu and I had made promises. We'd go to the same college. We'd room together. We had already picked the school—University of Wisconsin in Madison, because Lulu's father had gone there and always talked about how big and beautiful it was. Far enough away from Denver and this place. I'd have a new name. I'd be taller. But from the incubator till thirteen is a long, long time. She'd remember me.

And Grandma. She'd be there, too. She'd promised. She was going to make a coconut cake for me. There'd be one candle on it—marking the first day of the rest of my life.

10

I<small>T RAINED THE EVENING WE WERE TOLD TO</small> pick our new names. We'd been at the safe house for three weeks. That night, as the rain hammered against the thin windows, Cameron sat on the cheap sofa, her eyes on the television. I had read a book where a girl could stare so hard, a thing would catch on fire. First I stared at Cameron's neck. When she didn't move, I stared at her hands. Then her shoulder.

"Do you feel hot yet?" I asked.

"No."

"Now?"

"No, stupid."

"How about now?"

Cameron peeled her eyes away from the television. Mama had lifted her ban on it after me and Cameron watched the same video four times in a row.

"Can you believe this is happening?"

She had had a game the night we left and was still wearing the turtleneck from her cheerleading uniform when we got here. Now she was wearing it again. She'd had to leave the rest of it back in Denver. Her hair was a mess.

"Who cares?" I said.

Cameron rolled her eyes at me. "You're such a freak. You don't have the vaguest idea what this feels like. You can go to another place and make your one or two friends again. It's different for me. It's bigger."

"Yeah—a whole cheerleading squad. Whoopee."

"A whole *world*, stupid! You don't get it." She wiped her eyes quickly and glared at me. "You don't know anything, do you."

"It just . . . when I think about before, it . . . it hurts a lot. I can't be looking back right now."

Cameron looked at me for a minute and pushed some stray hairs behind her ear and let out a breath.

On the television, a woman was petting the leather interior of a Mercedes-Benz. The woman in the commercial looked at me and winked as though she and I were in on some secret. I threw my head back and laughed. Advertising was dumber than anything. The woman climbed out of the car and ran her hand over the top of it. I used to touch Matt Cat that way. The world was so stupid. The Feds had said no Matt Cat. No big reminders of who we once were. The whole world felt like it was dissolving. I petted the ugly couch the way the woman was petting the car.

"God, you're a freak!" Cameron said again.

"I heard you the first time, thank you very much."

"Well, you don't act like it, thank you very—"

"Stop it," Mama yelled from the bedroom where she was again poring over the literature she'd gotten from the Jehovah's Witnesses. "I'm getting sick of all your fussing."

I stuck my tongue out at Cameron. She mouthed *immature* and stared at the television.

"What's your name gonna be?" I asked, after a long time had passed.

"Cameron," she said. "The same name it's always been."

"It can't be, Cam. You know that."

A phone rang on the television, and Cameron jumped up then sat back down again. Except for the drivers' cell phones, which we weren't allowed to use, there wasn't a phone anywhere near us. No more raspy voice explaining exactly how it planned to kill us all.

"Anna," Cameron said softly, her voice breaking. "A palindrome. Backward and forward the same thing. Anna. Easy to spell. Easy to say. Easy to remember. Turn it completely around and it's the same thing." She swallowed and stared glassy-eyed at the television. "Anna," she said. "Forever and ever. Amen."

"Evie," I said, even though she hadn't asked. "Anna and Evie."

"Evie's a stupid name," Cameron said. "Why the hell would you call yourself that?"

I stared a fire into the side of her face, another into her elbow, a third into her thigh right where her stupid short skirt stopped and brown leg began. "It's mine," I said. "That's why."

"Oh—and that's supposed to be a good reason."

I closed my eyes and watched her burn.

PART TWO

11

I WANT TO TELL YOU WHERE WE ARE NOW, BUT I'm afraid. I want to say Toswiah and Cameron still *are*—only they're Evie and Anna now. World—please do remember me. I still *am*. Taller now. Still quiet. Sometimes I dance. Mama makes biscuits sometimes still. Even though she uses a mix now, I eat them the same way I always have—hot out of the oven, standing by the stove. Some days Anna still calls me immature. When we fight, Mama says *It's because you two are too close in age,* and Anna gets that look—her eyebrows shooting up and out like a bat's wings, her lips getting thin. *Fifteen months is fifteen months,* she says. *It makes all the difference.* Anna is fifteen. The school we're at now goes from sixth grade through twelfth. When Anna sees me in the hallways, she smiles and keeps walking. Even though she doesn't have many friends yet, she doesn't want to take the chance of being seen with someone in the lower school. Some evenings, I sneak her favorite sweater—the one with autumn colors in it, brown and gold and orange—out of the closet and into my knapsack. I don't put the sweater on until I'm in class, though. When I wear it, the girls in my class reach out to feel it and say nice things to me.

"Where'd you get it?" they ask.

"In San Francisco," I say. "Where I used to live."

Then someone always starts singing the Rice-A-Roni song from the old commercial they show on cable, until the others are laughing. *Rice-A-Roni, the San Francisco treat!* That's what people here know about San Francisco, the stupid commercial about a box of rice.

"There're other things there," I say. "Anyway, I don't even think Rice-A-Roni's made there!"

"What other things?" a girl named Toswiah asks, her eyebrows coming together all mean on her face. "You trying to say San Francisco's better or something?"

"No," I say, walking away, pulling the sweater tighter around me.

"I didn't think you were. That sweater might be cute, but that doesn't mean you get to start thinking you're better than anybody!"

Tonight I need to write. *"Afraid" is this hollowed-out place that sometimes feels bigger than I am. Most days my fear is as long as my shadow, as big as my family's closet of skeletons.*

Can you see me here?

A new girl comes to our class late in the year. I am in fourth grade. When people ask, we tell them we're cousins. The new girl has a bump on each hand where a sixth finger used to be. When the others point to it and laugh, she hides her hands behind her back. I get up and stand beside her, wanting them to stop. The girl's bottom lip trembles. "Whatever you do," I whisper to her, "don't let them see you cry." The girl smiles. It's a tiny, tiny smile. But I see it. Later I will touch the tiny bumps with my pointer finger and tell her to always think of them as beautiful.

Look for the beauty, my mama says. Always look for the beauty. It's in every single body you meet.

The girl smiles. She has a pretty smile.

12

THE TOSWIAH IN MY CLASS IS SMALL AND LOUD with a constant circle of friends around her. I have never heard this name before on another girl. When our teacher takes attendance, there is that split second when I believe that everything is back the way it once was. We both say *Here!* and Toswiah's friends look at me and laugh. I am Evie. I am Evie. I *am*. The other Toswiah doesn't look anything like me—she is shorter and round-faced with dimples and cornrows. I want to snatch her name away and press it all over myself. I want to hear people calling it—calling out to *me*. I would like for her or anyone to be the one that's disappeared.

At lunch today, Toswiah and her friends circled me in the school yard. It was cold out, gray. The ground was still wet from yesterday's rain. I was dressed in Denver clothes—a light green ski jacket and dark green pants. Toswiah and her friends dress like this place—dark colors with designer names showing everywhere.

"Where are you from again?" Toswiah asked. Her eyes narrowed, but her voice was soft. I stared at her, surprised.

"Bay Area." Around us, kids were chasing each other and laughing. There were a few couples leaning against the handball court making out. "San Francisco. You know—the Rice-A-Roni song thing."

Toswiah rolled her eyes at me. "Is everyone in the *Bay Area* named Toswiah, or do you just like answering to my name?"

"It's my cousin's name," I said, looking down at my hands. "I just haven't heard it on anybody else before. It makes me miss her."

Toswiah and her friends looked at me a long time.

Toswiah's nails are long, painted dark blue with a bright yellow sun on each one.

Mama's religion says *We are in the world but not of the world.* Maybe that's true. It's a religion of lots of rules that I don't believe in, but once in a while it makes sense. This place isn't my world. My soul isn't here. I bit my lip. Mama didn't want us to make friends. *It's too dangerous,* she said. *I know how you girls tell your friends every single thing. There'll be time for friends,* she said. *Let's just get ourselves good and settled in who we are first. If you're truly hungry for friends, make friends with the Witnesses.*

Ugh! Anna said. *And what? Party with the Bible on a Saturday night? I don't think so.*

"I was in San Francisco once," one of Toswiah's friends said. "It's a stupid place. Cold in the summer-time."

"The coldest winter I ever spent was a summer in San Francisco," Toswiah sang, like it was a rap song she'd just made up.

I smiled. "Mark Twain said that."

The other girls looked at me, but Toswiah's lips turned up a little. She shrugged.

"Maybe. Maybe not."

"It's pretty there, in San Francisco," I said.

"No, it's not," the girl said.

Toswiah rolled her eyes again. "Don't even go there, Tamara. You know she's a Joho, and Johos can't fight anybody. It's against their religion."

"My mother is," I said. "I'm not."

"Then why don't you pledge to the flag?"

"Because my mother doesn't allow us to."

"Mama's girl," Tamara said.

"Joho head," another girl said.

"So why'd you move here, then," Tamara asked, "if San Francisco's so pretty?"

We had been taught to say we moved here because we wanted a change. But standing there, that reason sounded stupider than anything. What kind of change? A gray, cold place where people thought we were weird?

"Just because," I said. "Why did your family move here?"

"I was *born* here," Tamara said. "And my mother and her mother and my father and his father." She circle-snapped her finger in front of my face, making the others laugh.

"My father read somewhere that this was a better place to live," I said. Across the yard, I could see Anna talking to a boy and laughing.

"It's the *only* place to live," Toswiah said.

"Oh," Tamara teased. "Like you've been everyplace else."

"I don't have to be everyplace else to know what's good."

If you'd ever been to Denver, I wanted to say, *you'd know there were better places.* But I stood there silently, trying to think of something else. Even thinking the word—*Denver*—brought tears to my eyes.

"Hey! There's Eric!" another girl said. Then Toswiah and the others were walking fast toward a group of boys.

I watched them walk away. A terrible loneliness came over me, making me shiver. When I looked up, the sky was almost silver. A beautiful, sad silver. All around me, kids were screaming and laughing and running. *"Denver,"* I said to the this-place sky. *"It's pretty there. We have the Rocky Mountains."*

The cold here is different. It slips into you gently, then makes its way deep inside. And settles. I pulled the zipper on my coat up to my neck, feeling the cold

air all the way to my bones. *Toswiah. I am Toswiah.*
Everyone around me had first names they'd been born
with and would probably carry to their grave.

The laughter and screaming grew further and further away from me.

I stared up at the sky and started spinning slowly,
not caring who was watching. I lifted my arms out beside me and threw my head back. The sky twirled dark
gray, then silver, then silver-white. I spun until I collapsed from spinning. Collapsed right onto the cold,
wet this-place ground. No one came over to lift me up
by my arms.

How could they when I wasn't even there?

13

In fifth grade I sat behind a girl named Carla. One morning, as I stared at the back of Carla's head, I saw a bug crawl down behind her ear and disappear into her thick brown hair. A few minutes later, another bug crawled across her neck. Carla reached up and scratched her head hard. When I saw the third bug, I screamed and pointed to it, yelling that Carla had head-bugs. Everyone in the class ran over and the teacher tapped her ruler on the desk for order. Carla put her head down on her desk and cried. That afternoon, our teacher sent notes home to everyone's parents telling them how they had to check our heads for lice. As my mother went through my hair with a hard plastic comb that night, I though about Carla. I knew by the next morning she would be the cootie-girl, and even as I kept hearing the awful, gulping sound Carla made as she cried, I couldn't help feeling relieved that it was her and not me.

Now I stood in the middle of the school yard, staring up at the sun. It was Monday, a month before my fourteenth birthday. The sky was bright blue. So bright, I had to squint to look at it. I was the cootie-girl here. No one ever said it. They didn't have to. People kept far away from me and laughed when I passed them in the hall. Once, I thought I saw Toswiah lifting her hand to wave at me. But as I lifted mine to wave back, her hand moved on up and smoothed her hair away from her eyes. I stopped waving then and put my hand in my pocket.

I took a notice out of my pocket and stared at it. In gym we'd been given permission letters to take home for different sports. I went down the list and stopped at TRACK & FIELD. In Denver, I could outrun most of the boys in my class but couldn't join the track team because it conflicted with hockey and basketball. But here—it felt like I'd been running forever, so why stop? I circled TRACK & FIELD, wondering if I wanted to do any other stuff. There was soccer, gymnastics, and tennis. No basketball. No hockey. I had always hated gymnastics, the way the girls had to move like butterflies all over everything. I wanted the sports that let me land hard and breathe loud. I scanned the school yard for Anna, wondering if she was somewhere looking at the list and cursing the fact that there was neither a cheerleading squad nor a basketball team. I didn't see her anywhere. I started to sign my father's name—Jonathan Green—then caught myself and signed his new name where it said PARENT'S SIGNATURE. I folded the paper and stuffed it into my knapsack.

Sometimes you dream, Anna said when I asked her how we'd ever keep doing this. *And sometimes you just cry. But when you stop crying and stop dreaming, it's all still here.*

We had been sitting in the bedroom. We could hear Mama and Daddy arguing outside our door. Their arguments had become familiar over the months. In Denver, when they used to kiss, I'd make a face and tell them how gross they were. Now, I would give *anything* to see my father pull my mother to him and hold her.

So you just think about the far, far future and do everything you can to make it feel like it's coming quick. You taught me that. Way back when I thought I could never get through this.

I did?

Yeah, Anna said. *How could you not remember that? I feel like it saved my life.*

Anna turned back to her science book then. She was studying hard and getting A's on all her tests. She was making friends at school. Not as many as she had in Denver, but people liked her. It was different here, though. She never brought her friends home or went to their houses. And nobody called. When she wasn't watching TV or doing her nails, she was studying. There was a college in Massachusetts—Simon's Rock—that you could go to at sixteen.

That's the prize I have my eyes on, Anna said. *A full ride there would mean no roadblocks. Nobody* saying "We can't afford it" or "God says blah, blah, blah, blah . . ."

When she starts talking about Simon's Rock, I want to say *What about me?!* And even though I never say it, Anna must see something in my eyes, because she always ends by saying *You'll get some-where, too, T. You might be a pain, but you've got a fire.*

The end-of-lunch bell rang and I headed slowly back into the building. Girls moved around me in groups and pairs, their arms around each other's waists and shoulders. Two guys in front of me slapped hands, promising to catch each other later, then headed off in separate directions down the hall. I had carried my knapsack out with me to study during lunch. Now I lifted it higher up on my back and thought about Lulu. Some days I could feel her—right there at my side, bumping shoulders with me. The two of us laughing. Lulu. I pulled my knapsack tighter to me and swallowed. Once she had said that my moving away was gonna leave a big hole in her life. Now I wondered if she had found someone else to be close to, if that hole had filled up and closed over. Even though I believed we'd meet again in college, sometimes *the missing* made me feel unsure. Now I was almost as tall as my mother. I wondered if Lulu had grown, too. Her mother would say *Look at Miss Toswiah—getting all tall on us.* And Lulu would laugh her laugh while I stood there in embarrassment. I would give anything for that moment. Absolutely positively anything.

14

It's Saturday. Outside it's cloudy and cold. The sky's still that weird silver-gray, the way it never got in Denver. I am fourteen today. When we left Denver I was almost completely flat. That's not the case anymore. My clothes from last year are too tight. The pants are all too short. The T-shirts curve over my chest in a way that makes the guys at school look twice. When the corner guys hanging out say *Hey Neckbone* to me, their voices have something else to them. Sometimes they even whisper *C'mon over here* in a way that makes me walk faster past them.

The coconut cake is store-bought with nothing written on it. *Fed money cake,* Anna said when she opened the refrigerator and saw the cake there. Once Mama had been a great cook. Now she cooked like she couldn't care less about the taste of anything. *Fed money everything.* The Feds send us a check every month—enough to pay rent and buy food and clothes until Daddy finds work. The money from our house is in the bank. Mama says when the time is right, we'll start looking for a place to buy.

Jehovah willing, she adds.

At night I ask her god to will us to a better place.

This morning, Mama is leaving, Bible in hand. She's going to spread the good news of Jehovah's coming kingdom. Mama's religion forbids celebrating birthdays. No candles on the cake this year. No singing "Happy Birthday." That's all behind us now. Lulu and I always found some way to be together on our birthday. Me, her and all of our friends. I want to call her now, say *Happy birthday, girlie.* Hear her say *Right back at you.* Same day, a few minutes apart. Less than five pounds. *You think we were together in another life?* she asked me once, her head on my shoulder.

Yeah, I said. *And then we traveled together to this one.* Another life. Another time. Lulu.

When I get to the University of Wisconsin, me, Lulu and Grandma will make up for all the birthdays we missed.

This morning, my father came into my room at dawn and said *Happy birthday, copper penny.* And for a moment, somewhere between waking and dreaming, I believed my father was well again and that we were back in Denver.

When I woke up, and saw we were still in this place, that my father was back at his chair by the window, I said *Pennies aren't made out of copper anymore! Don't you know that?!*

Daddy nodded, his eyes spilling over with sadness.

Sorry, I said.

I sat on his lap even though I am way too big for it, and Daddy put his arms around me, saying *I know, sweet Toswiah. I know.*

He smelled liked dirty clothes. I swallowed. He'd never smelled this way before. His hair was grown out and uncombed and his hands trembled when he hugged me. When he'd first started being this way, the

Feds had given Mama the name of a therapist to take him to. But Daddy stopped going or Mama stopped taking him—I don't know which. I hugged him tighter. He was right there but slipping away from me.

Daddy stared out the window without saying anything. I wanted to tell him he did the right thing, that it was better this way. I lay my head on his shoulder. It felt bonier than I remembered. His legs felt bony, too. Outside, the sky was off-white, like a dirty sheet had been laid across it. The words didn't come. We just sat there like two empty bags of skin and bone . . . staring at the dirty-sheet sky.

When was the last time you laughed, Daddy? I wanted to ask him. *It feels like a hundred years ago.*

Sometimes I'm so afraid in this place. Last night, we had Fruity Pebbles for dinner and only a little bit of milk. It feels like every day the world falls a little more apart. Once I had a mother and a father and we were all happy. Some days it felt like me and Anna in the world all by ourselves. And the world we're in doesn't make any kind of sense anymore.

"WHAT YOU NEED TO DO IS GET UP OUT OF THAT chair and get looking for a job," my mother says now.

Outside, it begins to rain softly. The sky drops a bit closer to the ground. Daddy's eyes move slowly from the rain to Mama and then back again.

"A job," my father says, his voice breaking. "A job?"

"Yes," Mama says. "You've been sitting at that window like some sick old man for all these months. Playtime is over. You should have thought about all you're thinking about before now. Made some other choices."

"Do you regret the choice we made?" he asks softly.

Anna lifts her face from her math textbook and looks at Mama, her eyes wide. "Say it," she whispers. "Say it!"

I'd give a thousand tomorrows, she said one night. *I'd give a whole ten years of my life to be back in Denver the way we used to be.*

Mama lifts her Bible to her chest and hugs it. After a long time has passed, she says, "You did the right thing."

Anna curses under her breath and turns back to her homework. This morning she gave me the autumn-colored sweater, kissed me on the forehead. Her lips felt strange. Good strange.

"I know how to be a cop," Daddy says. "I know what's right and what's wrong." He looks at each of us and nods. "Right and wrong," he says again, then turns back to the window.

"And I knew about Denver and teaching there," Mama says. "But all that's behind us now. Jehovah has a plan, and we have to—"

"What plan?!" my father shouts. Anna and I jump, but Mama stands there as if this loud voice came out of Daddy every single day. "What damn plan does your god have?! Tell me, because I want to be a part of it!"

Mama presses her Bible closer to her chest and doesn't say anything. She doesn't look angry. Just a little bit . . . a little bit broken.

"Don't take this away from me," she says. "Not this, too."

I lay my head down on the kitchen table. The pages of my notebook feel cool against my face. We're supposed to write a story about a dream we had that changed us. I've had three hundred dreams and still wake up in this tiny apartment in this world that doesn't have anything to do with us.

"I was a cop for fifteen years," my father says to the window. "Fifteen years! When I walk down these streets and see cops, I see that thing in their eyes that still believes in it. Still believes they can protect the world and change it and make it good. Well, you know what—I used to have those same beliefs, but they died with Raymond Taylor. They died the morning I walked into the D.A.'s office. They died when Randall and Dennis got sent to jail for manslaughter. *I* did that. I sent two cops to jail. Two *cops!* And it tore me up inside! Tore me up!"

Me and Anna sit straight up, our eyes wide. *They went to jail,* I think, feeling a smile coming on. The first few times we asked him, he wouldn't tell us, and then we were too scared to ask anymore. And now, here it was, in this tiny apartment all these miles away from Denver. They went to jail. When I look over at Anna, she's half-smiling, too. I hug myself hard, scared of my father's voice, so loud in the room, but loving the words coming out of his mouth. They went to jail!

He turns slowly and glares at my mother. "Do you know what that felt like? It felt like sending *myself* to jail. It didn't feel like the right thing no matter how many times you tell me it was. It felt as wrong as Raymond Taylor's dying felt! And so now what do I have? Tell me, Mrs. Thomas. Tell me what your god's next plan is, because I'm as tired of myself at this window as you are!"

Mama bites her bottom lip and stares at Daddy. The room is silent. It is the most he's said in a long time, and the words hit us all hard. Anna stares down at her hands. The smile is gone now, but she's not frowning, either. I put my braid in my mouth and chew the end of it for a minute. The apartment is dead silent. When my father sighs, I get up and put my arms around his shoulders. He reaches up and pats my hand absently. He is crying.

"I'm sorry," Mama says after a long time has passed. "I'm sorry it had to happen like this . . . to you . . . and to us." She sniffs and lets her breath out real slowly. "It's hard for all of us here, but we don't have to live this way."

Anna looks over at me and mouths *jail.* I nod. Even in this airless room, there is that tiny bubble of all-rightness. A tiny kernel of justice coming at us across all these miles.

Mama's voice softens. "In another month, I'll be certified to teach here and can start putting in applications at all the schools I can get to."

My grandmother taught. Mama says she never

thought of doing anything else. *Teaching's in my blood*, she said. *No*, she said. *Teaching is my blood. It's all of me.* The one thing the Feds screwed up on was my mother's teaching certificate. First they botched her name, then they forgot to send a new one. My mother believes it's because they didn't want her to teach for a while. For whatever reason, it was finally on its way.

At night, my mother studies the Bible the way she once pored over her daily lessons, marking passages, researching the origins of them and reaching further to understand and explain it all. Who was Judas, Job, Hotham the Aroerite, Salome, Apostle John? Where was Gomorrah, Canaan, the Black Sea, Babylon, Ephesus, Patmos? Ask Mrs. Thomas. She knows.

That night back in Denver when the raspy voice called, my mother screamed and the bite of jelly sandwich I had just swallowed lodged in my throat. When I see her sitting in the bedroom bent over the Bible, I can still feel it.

Mama's wearing one of her teacher dresses—the blue one with white piping along the bottom. She has lost weight over the months, and the dress sags at her waist and shoulders. Her hair is pulled back into a braid, pinned up at her neck. She is thirty-nine. Before all of this happened, she was making plans for her fortieth birthday party. Her invite list was two pages long. Her friends are gone now, too. Behind her. No contact. Mama looks down at her Bible. The Kingdom Hall is filled with new friends who call themselves her sisters and brothers. Mama goes every other night. On Sundays, me and Anna have to go with her. Her new sisters and brothers smile at us, don't ask questions about our before life. When they did, Mama said *It's nothing anyone needs to know about. Nothing even worth mentioning.* The sisters and brothers nodded as though they had lived their whole lives this way—full of things not worth mentioning. No one nosed too hard. *The future's what matters,* the Witnesses said. *Jehovah's plan.* It made me think that they were all hiding some part of themselves somewhere. Jehovah's Witnesses don't pledge to the flag. They don't celebrate holidays. They don't celebrate birthdays. *We're in the world but not of the world,* Mama says. *And anyway, a birthday is just another year.*

"A job," Daddy says again. He looks over at me, his eyes flickering recognition. "T," he says. "Anna?" Then his eyes flick off, away from me.

"Leave him alone, Mama," Anna says. And for a

moment, the old Anna—Cameron—is there, looking at Daddy, her face all bunched up with worry. But then, just as quickly, she frowns, sucks her teeth at him and turns back to her schoolbooks. At night, Anna says *If I ignore him, he'll go away. Like a rotten tooth.*

Where will he go? And I'm scared suddenly. Scared that Daddy will disappear as quickly and as permanently as Denver did.

And Anna shrugs, glares at me and says *Who cares. He ruined my life!*

Now Mama looks over at Anna and frowns. "I'll leave all of you alone!" She slowly puts on her raincoat, slips her Bible and some plastic-covered *Watchtowers* and *Awake!*s into her shoulder bag, and leaves.

I stare past Daddy's shoulder out the window. Outside, Mama takes the magazines out of her bag and walks slowly, holding them up to people she passes. The people shake their heads or ignore her. Their eyes flickering pity or disdain. Some look straight ahead like Mama's not even there.

Something's gone dead on Mama's face, like some part of her is remembering that this isn't who she always was. That she was once a teacher. That her students loved her. At the end of the school year, students would put so many apples and "World's Best Teacher" statues and mugs and T-shirts on her desk, we'd have to come help her carry all the stuff home.

She holds the magazines in front of her now. Maybe she thinks they'll keep the memories from coming. *Hello. May I bring you some good news today?* she says to the people she passes.

My father takes my hand and pulls each finger gently. He looks up at me and smiles. "Evie," he says, shaking his head and sighing. "My sweet copper piggy."

"Penny!" I say, looking at him sideways, not sure if he knows he's made a mistake.

But then he smiles slowly and pulls my pinky finger. "And this little penny stayed home," he says, winking at me.

Then I laugh, relieved. He and I stare out the window, our shoulders touching. He needs a bath. But beneath that smell, there is the smell that has always been Daddy.

"I'm glad Randall and Dennis went to jail," I whisper.

My father pulls my head to his shoulder and sighs. The rain falls and falls. Mama holds the *Watchtower*s up a little higher and walks on.

The walls in Mama's classroom are covered with photographs of her students. Not the regular class pictures, but pictures of them with their families, them on bikes and roller skates, in swimming pools and on swing sets. In the photos the kids are always laughing. Sometimes they're looking at the camera and sometimes they're not. I walk slowly along the walls while Mama teaches. Her students watch her, listen intently, ask questions, sneak looks at me. "Mrs. Green—is that really your daughter?" they ask when Mama stops for a moment and says, "I know you have questions about that girl walking around the class, so go ahead and ask them!" She smiles when she says this, gives me a sly look. I feel grown-up—like me and Mama are in on some secret the rest of the kids are too young to understand. In a week I'll be thirteen and everything—good and bad these days, seems to make me cry. Mama calls it "the tears of thirteen," tries to get me to laugh at how easily the tears come. This afternoon she's taking me shopping for a birthday outfit. Outside, the sky is blue and cloudless. Mama's students look at me in wonder, their mouths slightly open. "Mrs. Green," a boy with brown hair and glasses says, "she only looks a little bit like you." I lean against the wall of pictures and fold my arms. Their faces reveal their love for Mama—the way their eyes fill up with pride when she singles them out for something good, the way they look away in shame when she scolds them, the way they rush to be the student standing closest to her when she calls them over to a map spread out on her desk. I look at Mama and feel a rush of pride and love so deep, I have to tilt my head back to keep the tears from coming.

15

TOSWIAH'S DRESS IS GREEN AND TIGHT AND comes down past her ankles. It is sunny out, cold but not freezing. When she starts walking toward me, the dress seems to float out behind her. Lulu had a dress like that, and when Toswiah's dress lifts up in the wind, tears start stinging. I bite my bottom lip and look away from her, but she keeps coming.

"You said you had a cousin named Toswiah? What was she like?"

Her voice isn't mean when she asks this, just curious. And for the first time, I think that maybe she be-lieves me.

I shrug. "She was nice," I say, thinking of Lulu. "I miss her a lot."

"She doesn't visit you?"

"Uh-uh."

Toswiah lets out a loud breath. When I look at her, she's taking in the whole school yard, like the answers to everything are out there somewhere.

"Well, why the hell not?"

"Her mother and my mother are sisters. But they don't speak. They had a fight a long time ago about I don't know what. And that was the end." I look at her and pull my lips to the side. The lie comes as easily as water.

"My mom has a sister that lives down South. She can't stand her," Toswiah says. "Grown-ups can be so stupid. That's your sister, right?" She points across the school yard to where Anna's standing with two other girls.

I nod.

"My sister's retarded," Toswiah says. She looks at me, one eyebrow raised.

I smile. "I think mine is, too."

Toswiah shakes her head. The dress blows up a little, and she flattens it down against her legs with both hands. "No. I mean really retarded. Only everybody calls it 'developmentally disabled.' Only that's too long to say. She's seventeen."

I don't know what to say, so I don't say anything. We stare out at the school yard without saying anything.

After a moment, Toswiah says, "Well, I'll see you later."

I lift my hand and wave at her even though she's standing close enough to touch.

"See you later."

She stands there another minute like she's waiting for me to say something else.

"Thanks," I say.

"For what?"

I shrug and sort of smile. "For, you know. Coming over to talk to me."

Toswiah looks at me for a long time. "Whatever," she says. Then slowly walks away. When she gets halfway across the school yard, she turns and waves back.

I watch the wind lift her dress up around her ankles. It's a warm wind, gentle. I feel it in my hair and against my ears. Maybe it's a warm front. Coming in from Colorado.

16

On Sunday, my mother got up early and started fussing about me and Anna not going to Kingdom Hall enough. Anna put the pillow over her head and cursed. I sat up in bed and stared outside. Christmas lights flashed from people's windows. We would not be celebrating Christmas this year or any holiday in our mother's house ever again.

On Thanksgiving, Mama made lasagna and thanked her Jehovah for giving us another day. We ate the lasagna quietly, listening to Mama preach about how worldly holidays were wrong. *I don't know how celebrating the fact that Pilgrims and Native Americans stopped fighting long enough to sit down and eat a meal together is a sin in God's eyes,* Anna had said. I had never been a big turkey fan, but I missed Thanksgiving, missed all the people who stopped by to eat dinner or dessert with us and wish us a happy holiday. I missed us putting up lights two days after Thanksgiving and me and Anna fighting over how we'd hang them.

Now I stared out the window, wondering if those houses with lights had trees up already and if there were presents under them. The Christmas before last, I'd gotten so much stuff, I thought I'd never stop unwrapping. Most of it was still in Denver somewhere. Stuffed animals, games, clothes, gone. Even the ring Daddy had given me with TOSWIAH engraved into the gold.

I bit my lip, feeling the tears coming on. *Don't think about the past,* Anna said. *Just the far, far future.* The sky was overcast. We'd been here over a year and I still didn't know if that meant rain or snow. The windows rattled, which was a sure sign that it was freezing outside. I climbed out of bed slowly and stuck my feet into the ugly pink bedroom shoes Mama had gotten us.

"Get up, Anna. You hear Mama fussing. You know this means we gotta go to Kingdom Hall today."

Anna groaned and rolled over toward the wall. Her side of the room was neater than mine. There were pink frilly things on her dresser and posters of musicians on her side of the wall. I didn't listen to much music anymore.

"You stay in bed too long, you know she'll pick out your outfit."

Anna rolled back over and opened her eyes. "I hate this life!" she said. "Hate it!"

"Far, far future," I said. Anna glared at me.

Every now and then Mama started making noise about how we'd all be destroyed in Armageddon if we didn't straighten up and fly right. The first time she said it, Anna said *It'd be better than what I have now*, and Mama fussed at her for so long, I'm sure Anna was sorry she'd ever opened her mouth to say anything. Ever since then, Mama only once in a while made us go to Kingdom Hall. But when she did, there was no arguing with her about it.

I went over to the closet and pulled out a green wool jumper. Women weren't allowed to wear pants at Kingdom Hall because the elders said it was being disrespectful to God—which made no sense to me. I mean, Eve was hopping around the Garden of Eden *naked* and God didn't seem to be mad about that. I didn't believe a whole lot that the religion said, but sometimes they hit on something that made me go "Oh." Like once, this guy was giving a sermon about the Ten Commandments. I'd never really paid attention to them before, but when he was reciting them, they made sense—I mean, basically, they're just saying be nice to people if you want people to be nice to you. It made me wish I hadn't pointed to Carla's lice-filled head all those years ago—giving her a first-class ticket to cootie-land.

Jehovah's Witnesses believe you go back to the dust after you die—that it's like you never were. They believe a few people go to heaven and some go to the New World that God's gonna create after He gets tired of how messed up this one is. No hell, though. Heaven, New World, or dust—those are your options.

Toswiah and Cameron? Dust. Evie and Anna? New

World. Daddy? Already living in another religion's hell. Mama? Heaven? Who knows.

Mama says in the New World, there won't be any more hatred or disease or floods. She says the animals will all be friendly. *You'll be able to pet snakes and hug lions,* she says, her eyes getting bright.

I pulled a dark green turtleneck off the hanger, got some underwear out of the drawers that Anna and I shared—she had the two top ones and I had the two bottom—then headed off to the bathroom, mumbling good morning to Mama and Daddy as I went past.

Our bathroom here is tinier than the downstairs *half*-bathroom we had back in Denver and three times as small as the upstairs bathrooms. I'd never thought of us as rich when we lived there, but now I know we had it good. I closed the door, pressed my head against the cool mirror glass and sighed.

When I came out, Daddy was sitting at the window, eating a bowl of oatmeal. He looked over at me and smiled.

"Your sister up?" Mama asked. She was pouring pancake mix from a box into a white plastic bowl. In Denver, all her mixing bowls had been the good kind, made out of glass. Here, everything except Daddy's oatmeal bowl seemed plastic and cheap and temporary.

I nodded and took another step before stopping. "Mama," I said, turning slowly toward her. "It's all wrong, isn't it?"

Daddy put his oatmeal bowl down in his lap and stared out the window. I swallowed. "This wasn't how it was supposed to end."

Mama poured water into the batter and stirred. "What's guaranteed, Evie?"

I shrugged.

"Nothing's guaranteed, honey. Nothing. If someone tells you something is, don't believe it."

"But I thought—"

"Did you thank Jehovah for allowing you to wake up this morning?" Mama asked.

Anna sat down across from me at the kitchen/dining room/den table and made a face. She was wearing a wool skirt that stopped at her ankles and a light blue sweater that looked about two sizes too small. Where I'd gotten taller over the year, Anna had just gotten bigger—not fat, but every part of her body seemed to be "blooming into womanhood," as Mama liked to say.

Mama sat down next to me and put a plate of bacon in the middle of the table. I looked at her sideways. Every day I hoped that she would say "Psyche your mind. I was just kidding about the God stuff," but it never happened. If anything, she got *holier*.

"Well, did you? Either of you?"

"I did," I lied.

"Yeah," Anna said. "Me, too. Like I do every day."

Mama raised an eyebrow at her but didn't say anything.

Anna took a bite of bacon.

"Are you going to say the blessing?" Mama asked.

Anna bowed her head. "ThankyouJehovahforthisfoodandallotherblessingsamen."

I laughed, then covered my mouth with my hand.

Mama took a sip of her coffee. "I don't think it's asking a whole lot to be thankful for what we have," she said quietly, looking from me to Anna. "Sometimes I think if we'd been more thankful—more *aware* of what we had in Denver—things wouldn't have ended the way they did."

Anna and I looked at each other but didn't say anything. My mother hardly ever mentioned Denver. When she did, we knew we'd taken something too far.

"I think the road back is a narrow one," she said. "A part of me believes that if we do everything right, we can have it again."

"But we can't ever go back there."

"Not Denver," Mama said. She looked over at my father sitting by the window and lowered her voice. "The happiness. It's not always going to be like this."

It all seemed too vague. I wanted definite. Either we got back to Denver or we didn't. Either we were happy or we weren't. Jehovah's Witnesses believe that their religion is the true one and that they're the chosen people. Well, that's what I wanted—the truth. Who were we really? And why? Why had this had to happen to us? Why couldn't someone else's daddy have witnessed the murder?

"What about babies?" I asked, wanting to change the subject. "With this Armageddon thing, the end of things that you always talk about, will babies get destroyed, too—because they can't walk, so they can't go out in field service and pray and stuff?"

Mama frowned at me, checking my face to see if I was messing with her. I wasn't. We could start at the beginning—the basics. Who was this god of hers, anyway? Why would He want to destroy babies—and families?

"Jehovah can see into people's hearts," Mama said. "He knows who's who and who's going to be who."

"How come He didn't give Hitler a disease or something?" Anna asked. "To keep him from killing all those Jews? Or what about the people who killed Martin Luther King Jr. and the Kennedys? And Malcolm X? What about those guys? Or like when—"

"Or what about us?" I yelled. "What about *us?* What did we do to deserve this?!"

Mama shook her head. "The Lord works in mysterious ways. He has His plans and it's not for us to understand. There's a reason why we're here. We just don't know it yet."

She bit her bottom lip, her eyes glazing over. After a moment she blinked and looked from me to Anna. In that split second, I saw her again—the lady I used to know in Denver. My mother.

"You're strong," she said. "You're both so strong." She bit her lip again. "My strong, strong daughters . . ." Her voice trailed off.

"I don't want to be strong!" Anna said. "I just want . . . I just want to be who I am! Who I always was!"

Mama smiled. It was a small smile, but I saw it. I remembered it. From a long time ago.

"No one can take that away," she said, her voice no more than a whisper. A moment passed before she added my sister's name. "Cameron."

Anna and I looked at her, our mouths open. How long had it been since I'd heard that name coming from her mouth? I blinked slowly. When I looked at Mama again, her eyes were far off and she was our new mother again. But Anna was smiling.

Mama's Bible was sitting beside her plate. She picked it up and begin reading. " 'Even though I walk in the valley of deep shadow, I fear nothing. . . .' "

"I need new running sneakers," I said.

Mama ignored me and kept reading. " 'Surely goodness and loving-kindness will pursue me all the days of my life.' "

"I think God will see it loving and kind of you to let me get a good day's sleep. So I should be able to get right back to bed now instead of—"

"You're coming today, Anna," Mama said. "You just got new sneakers, Evie."

I bit the inside of my lip. It felt like the moment when she said Anna's old name had never happened.

"They're too heavy."

"Too heavy for what?"

"They make my knees hurt," I said quickly. This wasn't a total lie. What I had were cross-trainers, and even a nonprofessional like me knew real runners had real running shoes, not cross-trainers. Cross-trainers would definitely mess up your knees if you ran too much in them.

Anna frowned at me. A "Yeah, right" frown. A "What are you up to now?" frown.

"And plus," I added, "they feel too tight now."

"We'll get you new sneakers, then," my father said from the window.

"I need new sneakers, too," Anna said.

"You can have mine. I hardly wore them."

"Yuck!" Anna took a tiny bit of bacon and glared at me. "I don't want your skanky sneakers."

"I don't know what I'm going to do with you two," Mama said. "Just eat and hush." But there was a small, proud smile at the edge of her mouth.

I watched our father staring up at the overcast sky as if some big answer was about to drop out of it into the empty bowl on his lap. He was disappearing. Sitting at the living room window, but disappearing. The papers Mama had brought home were piling up beside his chair. She had opened them to the want ads. They lay there, right where she had left them. Untouched.

Mama looked at her watch and told us to finish eating and get our coats. She got up from the table and went over to the bookshelf for our Bibles. Anna chewed her bacon slowly. She put her finger to her lips.

"Hush," Anna said. "Just hush."

I half-smiled, not sure what she was trying to say. But her eyes were serious.

Anna leaned across the table. "Make believe none of it ever happened," she said. "Hush. Make believe we never were. You and me, li'l sis, back to the dust."

Daddy looked over at us, lifting his bowl toward us like an offering. Anna sucked her teeth, got up and took Daddy's bowl to the kitchen.

Outside, I looked up at Daddy's window and waved. His hand lifted into the air absently.

I bent my head down against the cold and walked a little bit behind Mama and Anna. Our Bibles are green with HOLY SCRIPTURES written on them in gold lettering. When I held it away from me and squinted, it became a mountain in Denver.

Anna turned and saw me. "God, you're such a freak!"

I stared at her but didn't say anything. *Does it matter what I am*, I wanted to scream, *if I'm not anyone?!*

As Mama led us through the neighborhood, I watched people watching us and wondered who they saw.

Curl your toes into the soft pine of your floorboards. And do remember me.

PART THREE

17

THE COACH IS TALL AND SKINNY. HE TELLS US
we can call him Leigh. When he looks at my permission slip, he nods and asks if I'm related to Anna.

"She's my sister," I say, looking away from him. It
is Tuesday. Late afternoon. The school hallway is quieter than anything. My mother thinks I am getting tutored in science, because she wouldn't approve of track.
Not now. Not as a Witness. Her new motto is Acade-
mics and the Bible. So what if your body went to hell?
Your soul and brain would be fine. When I asked her
about getting tutored, she said *Why can't Anna help*

you? and Anna rolled her eyes and said *Because I've already forgotten the stuff she's just learning.*

This is the first big lie I've ever told her. It came easily.

"I teach geometry, also," Leigh says now. "Anna's one of my best students. Is she not a runner?" He smiles at me. One of his front teeth overlaps the other in a nice way. His running shoes look old but like a long time ago they were decent.

I am wearing my new ones and dark blue running pants with bright green stripes down the side. The white T-shirt I'm wearing used to say DENVER MIDDLE SCHOOL, but the letters are so bleached and faded, Mama had okayed me bringing it to this place. The shirt is soft and still smells faintly of our old house.

"Nah. She's not really into sports."

"Well, let's see if *you* are."

I follow him into the gym, where four girls are running in a line, one behind the other, passing a silver baton back and forth. When the one behind calls "Stick!" the one right in front of her throws her hand back. They do this a bunch of times, their motions smooth as water.

Above us, a line of girls are running around a track.

The track rail circles the whole gym. I can hear them breathing. Their feet pounding together sound like two huge feet instead of many. My own heart speeds up. Everyone seems to be connected to one another, in unison. I feel myself wanting this so hard, I have to bite my lip to keep from screaming out.

"You ever run track before?" Leigh asks.

I shake my head.

"Well, you'll need a pair of running shorts, spikes and flats—those are shoes for the track, you can get them at any good sports store. You'll also need—"

"We . . . I don't know if my parents can afford to—"

Leigh nods and blows the whistle hanging around his neck. The other girls stop running and begin to jog over toward us. He leans into me and says, "I'll need your clothing and shoe sizes."

I don't realize how tense my stomach is until it starts relaxing.

After everyone introduces themselves, Leigh asks the girls from last year to talk about the team. We sit down on the gym floor in a circle. I recognize two girls from my homeroom and a few others from seeing them around school.

"It's a good team," one of the girls, who introduced

herself as Mira, says. She is about my height, dark like my mother and soft-spoken. She speaks with a little bit of an accent. Like someone from England.

"We win a lot," a girl named Denise says. The others slap each other five and hoot.

I hug myself. The gym is big and chilly. My new running shoes feel stiff and wrong. All the others are wearing shoes like Leigh's—Adidas with thick soles and fluorescent stripes. The ones Mama has gotten me are a dark blue, no name brand that I have ever seen on anybody's feet before. I sit cross-legged and try to cover my feet with my hands.

"Okay, let's get to running," Leigh says. Everyone jumps up as though they've been stuck with pins.

When I am the last one to rise, Leigh says, "Fast, Evie. We do everything fast around here."

"So you're a runner," Mira asks me as we jog around the track. The track is an eighth mile around and banked at the curves. Leigh said we had to run a half mile at our own pace, but everyone takes off like it's a race, and by the second time around, I am struggling to keep breathing.

"I don't think so," I say, my voice coming hoarser than I've ever heard it.

"Your legs are long," Mira says. She smiles and pulls up to the front of the group. I take a deep breath, feeling warm. My legs are long, I keep thinking. Yes. Yes. My legs are long. It is the friendliest thing anyone has said to me in a long time.

"WHY ARE YOU SO SMELLY?" ANNA ASKS WHEN I get home. She is sitting at the kitchen table, studying, and I race by her to get a glass of water. I gulp it down without saying anything to her, then go over to the window and kiss my father. Mama is at Kingdom Hall. Tuesday night is her Bible study.

The last time Mama asked me and Anna if we wanted to go, Anna said *Are we gonna be tested on it?*

Mama lifted both hands and said *I give up. I'll miss you all in the New World.*

When you get there, pet a friendly lion for me, Anna mumbled. But not loud enough for Mama to hear.

I touch my face now. It feels warm and flushed. I'd run all the way home. In the cold air, it felt like I was breaking every speed limit. Like I could run all the way back to Denver.

"Why are you standing there *touching* yourself?" Anna asks, her voice rising with disgust.

I take my hand off my face and glare at her.

"Man," she says. "Take *me* to that study group!" Then she turns the page in her textbook and puts her head down on her arm to read.

"Was it helpful?" my father asks, his voice so soft, I can barely hear him.

"Very! It meets three times a week. I'm gonna keep going."

"Three times a week!" Anna says. "What are you trying to do—get the freaking *Nobel Prize*?!"

I sit down across from her. "Maybe."

"You have lost your mind."

I lift my arm and fan the sweat in her direction.

Anna throws a pen at me. But she's smiling.

18

LATER, LONG AFTER EVERYONE HAS GONE TO bed, I tiptoe into the living room and sit cross-legged on the floor. The moon, coming in through Daddy's window, is bright and halfway pretty. I try to remember Denver, how I used to spend hours staring out my window wanting to drink every ounce of its beauty in. Maybe I knew, someplace deep, that the day would come when it wouldn't be mine anymore. I swallow, remembering the morning I told Lulu. A part of me thought our tears were just for drama, that we'd wake up the next morning and everything would be back to normal. But as we lay across my bed, staring up at the ceiling and crying silently, the realness of how everything you ever loved could be taken away from you just like that settled over me, eerie and dangerous as quicksand.

Every month, a letter comes from Grandma. It comes in a white business envelope with a Texas postmark. We read the letters hungrily, over and over again. Sometimes, I come in to find Mama fingering the letter lovingly, a faraway look in her eyes. That's it. That's all we have left of the past. Letters with no names on them, just paragraphs and paragraphs of chatty news. No real questions about our lives, no news of what happened after we left, who asks about us, who calls her up to cry. When we write back, we're not allowed to use our new names. Our letters to her are guarded and shallow. Mama talks about Jehovah's will, me and Anna talk about the movies we saw, the classes we have. We can't describe our school, we can't talk about this new place. Our letters go to Texas and eventually get to her. What do we get—all of us? The knowledge that we're all alive. That somewhere beneath all the stupid shallow stuff, we're surviving. That we still love and are loved. That underneath this new Evie skin, there is still Toswiah Green. Some-where.

Always.

I stretch my legs out in front of me and bend slowly toward them the way Leigh showed me. I can feel the backs of my legs burning with the stretch. Leigh said this was a good thing, that in no time I'd be able to touch my forehead to my knees. I'm not the fastest girl on the team, but I'm not the slowest. After practice yesterday, a few girls came over to me and slapped my hand, welcoming me.

Daddy longlegs, Mira said when she waved good-bye. *Spider woman.*

Later, Spider, someone else said.

I lifted my head, then bent down toward my knees again, breathing out slowly.

Spider. I liked that.

19

When I walk in on Thursday, Mama is grinning and dancing around the room. I pull my knapsack off my shoulder, thinking that she's joined Daddy in the mind-loss game, but then she dances over to me and in her eyes, I see my old Mama, the one who let Daddy pull her up from her place on a picnic blanket and dance her around the park. When I look over at the table, Anna is sitting there smiling.

"She hasn't gone crazy," Anna says, reading my mind. "She just got a job."

Mama dances the letter into my hands. *Dear Mrs.*

Thomas: Let me be the first to congratulate you on your appointment at Public School 13 here in . . . I feel the room getting smaller, around then bigger again, the air coming fast into my throat. Maybe a part of me had thought it would never happen, that Mama would never walk into a classroom again and begin the day with "Good morning, children."

"Fifth grade," Mama says, still grinning. "I thought I'd have to teach high school. Thank you, Jehovah! Thank you for my faith."

Daddy stares out the window. Silent.

"Dance with her, Daddy," I say, wanting him to be smiling, too, happy for Mama. In Denver, when Mama told stories about her class, he'd throw his head back and laugh, happy. Proud.

I take Mama's hand and dance with her for a moment. Her hand is soft. The way I remember it, our feet moving in unison, Mama smiling.

"Like this, Daddy. That silly Hustle dance that you guys used to do."

Mama shakes her head, looks at the letter again and grins. She holds the letter in one hand and spins me with the other, then our feet come back into step together. After dinner some nights, they would put on music and dance like crazy, Daddy's feet moving faster than the music, Mama doing steps that looked like they were halfway cool once upon a time. And they'd laugh and pull us into them and we'd all just act the fool while somebody sang about love or zodiac signs or about white boys playing funky music.

But Daddy just keeps staring out the window. And after a moment, the room feels hollow. Mama squeezes my hand once, then lets it go, picks up the *Watchtower* on her way into their bedroom and closes the door behind her.

20

ON FRIDAY, SOMEBODY CALLED MY NAME. I turned and saw Mira running toward me. She was smiling.

"God, you walk fast, girl. Where you heading?"

I told her where I lived and slowed down a bit.

"You can keep walking fast," she said. "I can keep up, you know." She smiled again and took three giant steps out in front of me. "Spider woman. That's what you are for sure."

"Am not," I said, my heart beating fast. "I'm just a girl named Evie from California."

"California, huh?"

"Yep."

"Well, in California, can they run as fast as girls from Antigua?"

I lifted my knapsack higher on my shoulder, looked at her sideways and took off.

Mira laughed and ran to catch me. We ran to the corner, me getting there only a half second before her even though I'd had a head start.

Mira leaned over, her hands on her knees. I did the same thing. We were both breathing hard, laughing.

"Nah, man," Mira said between breaths. "I don't think the California girls got anything on Antigua!"

On Friday, Mira called my name. *Evie!* she said. *Evie, wait up a minute.*

Evie!

And for a minute, or maybe a hundred minutes— it was the most beautiful name in the world.

21

"What's the thing you ever wanted most in the world?" Anna asked me.

It was Saturday. Mama had given us money to go see a movie and get lunch somewhere. Even though it was two days into December, it was warm enough for us to unzip our ski jackets and stuff our scarves into our knapsacks. *Indian summer*, Anna had said, sniffing the air like a dog.

We were walking along a wide avenue. Fancy stores were on both sides of the street. Anna stopped in front of one where, on the other side of the glass, a bright red dress with sequins lay draped across a blue velvet chair. The window was covered with yellow cellophane—the kind we used to line our Easter baskets with. I lifted my knapsack higher on my shoulders, holding the straps so tight, my fingers hurt. Easter. Every holiday we ever celebrated felt like a long time ago.

"The thing I ever wanted most in the world?" I said, turning away from the window. "Not that dress."

"No, that's not what I mean, Evie." Anna caught up to me and linked her arm through mine. She was being friendly. Too friendly. It made me wonder what she wanted. There wasn't a single thing I could imagine her wanting from me. What I wanted most right then was to break into a run. I wanted to feel the wind fighting me—the way it did when we sprinted outside. I wanted to beat it, push against it like Leigh yelled for us to do, gliding past the relay team and Mira and Denise. I had been going to track practice for three weeks, and in that short time I had gotten faster. *Don't let your hands go past your hipbone*, Leigh had said. *Bring them right back up to your chest. Hip-chest. Hip-chest.* Some nights I dreamed I was lifting off, taking these huge strides past everybody I knew—Mama with her *Watchtower*, Daddy in his chair, Anna with all of her books, Toswiah and Tamara. Then I'd be back in Denver, and in the distance, Grandma and Lulu would be waving. But as I got closer to them, my stride got longer and I'd move right past them, struggling to stop but not able to. On those nights, I woke up startled, staring around our bedroom, wide-eyed and scared.

"Are you even listening to me?" Anna sounded annoyed. "Right here." She poked me in the center of my chest.

"Ouch!"

"What do you want right there?"

"Well, right now I want my sternum to stop hurting."

Anna rolled her eyes.

"You know what I want, Anna. What you want. What Mama wants. What Daddy wants. I want to be back in Denver!"

Anna smiled. Satisfied. "And if you couldn't have that?"

We passed a group of girls walking arm in arm. Anna and I looked at them without saying anything.

People were out doing Christmas shopping. Some of the girls had brightly colored shopping bags hanging from their shoulders.

"You asked me what I wanted more than anything. Not what I wanted if I couldn't have that."

"Well, now I'm asking you the other thing." She was grinning.

"What?!" I asked. "What is it?"

"Answer me!"

She stopped. This morning, she had taken her braid out, and now the wind whipped her hair in front of her eyes. She brushed it back and kept grinning at me.

"To belong somewhere, then," I said. "Or something like that. You know. To feel connected."

"Like the far, far future had come already, right?"

"Right."

We started walking again. At the corner, Anna stopped in front of a coffee shop. "Let's go in here," she said. "*We* need to talk, and *I* need something warm to drink."

I stopped walking. "About what?"

Anna grabbed my arm. "Just about," she said. "C'mon, girlie."

The coffee shop was crowded. Anna led us to a

table in the back, where we sat down and ordered chamomile tea—the one hot drink we both loved because the honey and chamomile together reminded us of Denver in the springtime.

When the waitress brought our tea, Anna looked at me.

"T," she said. She only used my old name when she was really happy or wanted to get something out of me.

"No," I said.

"I'm not asking you for anything. I need to tell you something. The far, far future came two days ago."

"What are you talking about, Anna?" I felt itchy suddenly. And scared.

Anna took a long white envelope from her knapsack and handed it to me. When I saw SIMON'S ROCK COLLEGE written on it, my hands starting shaking so bad, I could barely pull the letter from it.

"*Dear Miss Thomas*," I read slowly. "*We are very happy to inform you—*"

"I'm in!" Anna yelled, then quickly lowered her voice. "I am in there and. Out. Of. Here!"

"Anna," I said, feeling the wind go out of me, "what's going on?"

"I applied. I went ahead and did it, not thinking—I mean, *hoping* but not thinking it would hap—"

"But I thought you had to be . . . I thought you had to be sixteen!"

"I was wrong." Anna was still grinning, but I didn't see what there was to be all smiley about. "Not only do they have early acceptance, but you only need two years of high school—and to be an A student. And since we couldn't get those stupid Feds to change our school grades, the ones they sent to our school here were still kind of shaky. So I wrote a long essay about why it's so important for me to get out of here." She leaned in closer and the grin disappeared. "I told them, T. I used fake names and a different state, but I told them everything."

"But what about Officer Randall and—" I stopped suddenly, remembering the morning my father had told us that they had gone to jail. It seemed like forever ago.

Now Anna puffed out her cheeks and exhaled. She looked away from me, her eyes seeming to rest on everybody in the diner before she spoke. When she started talking again, her voice was low. She wouldn't look at me. "They've either got people still looking for us or they don't." She shrugged. "We're either gonna die because of this or we'll live. The way I figure it is, I want to live, I mean really live until the next thing happens." When she looked at me, her eyes were watery. "You've got track—"

I grabbed her arm hard. "What are you talking about?"

Anna pulled away from me and rubbed the place I'd grabbed. "Jeez. Calm down! Mr. Lacori—Leigh—told me. He said you had promise and stuff. He said you were fast. Don't worry. I won't say anything to anybody. I just don't know why you didn't tell me. It's not like I wouldn't have kept it secret."

"I don't know what you're talking about. I don't even know who this Mr. Lacori is." I felt my heart moving all over the place, felt like the words were falling over themselves to get out of my mouth. If she tried to take this away, I didn't know what I'd do. I hated her! Hated her!

"Stop lying, T," Anna said. "Why do you think you have to lie to me? You know exactly what I'm talking about. Track! Coach *Leigh Lacori.*" Her voice got softer. "You don't have to lie to *me,* T. We're on the same side of the fence."

I shrugged and looked away from her.

"It's mine!" I said, not caring that I sounded like a four-year-old. "Track's mine. And you and Mama and Daddy aren't gonna take it away from me. Nobody's gonna take it away from—"

"Nobody's trying to," Anna said. She tried to make eye contact, but I bit my lip and looked away from her. It felt like everything was falling apart. Slipping away.

"All I'm saying is, Mama and Daddy aren't gonna get us out of this one. We're in it together and we got to do it ourselves. You'll run. I'll go to Simon's Rock. Nobody's gonna stop either of us."

"If we're in it together, then how come you're thinking about leaving without me?"

"Because . . . because I know you're gonna be okay."

We drank our tea and didn't say anything for a long time. People came and went. The waitresses rushed past us, looking tired and harried.

"Do you ever think about that boy, T?"

When I didn't answer, Anna just kept talking.

"What do you think about him? I mean really, really think. Not just what comes across your mind once in a while, but in your gut. What do you think about

146

him way late at night when your mind's too tired to flick itself away from thinking too deep?"

I looked down at the letter. *We are very happy to inform you. We are very happy to inform you. We are very happy to inform you.* "I don't know. When you turned fifteen, I remember thinking that you were the age he was when he died. Sometimes I wonder where he was thinking about going to college or whether his schoolteacher mom still taught. Mostly, I just wish it never would have happened." I moved my finger slowly around the rim of my mug and thought for a moment. "Or that Daddy hadn't been there."

Anna stared at me. With her hair out and the makeup she had sneaked on after we left the house, she looked older. She had started dressing like the other kids at school, in tight, cropped sweaters, designer pants and high-soled shoes that made her taller than I was.

"When I was applying to Simon's Rock," she said, "I wrote about him. I talked about how Mama's religion says we go back to the dust, but I don't know if I believe that, because I feel the boy with me all the time. How at first I used to think it was so, so crazy—us, the innocent ones, having to leave because of some messed-up stuff the cops did. But now I think of it as part of a plan—a bigger plan. I don't know if it's God's or the universe's or Raymond Taylor's or fate's, but I feel like . . ." She leaned across the table, running her hand lovingly over the letter. "I feel like whatever it is, is way bigger than we are."

The waitress came over and asked us if we wanted anything else. I shook my head, but Anna ordered another cup of tea. The waitress gathered up our cups, looking annoyed.

"And a check, please," Anna said sweetly.

After the waitress left again, Anna picked up the letter. "Listen. This is the important part. *While we cannot offer you a full scholarship at this time, Simon's Rock can offer a two-thirds scholarship. You may also be eligible for our work-study program . . .*"

I sniffed, wiped my nose with the back of my hand.

"T," Anna said, looking up from the letter. "Don't. Come on, girlie. Be happy for me. You can visit me there, you know. Every weekend if you want. It's only three hours away." She touched my hand across the table. I snatched it back from underneath hers and quickly wiped my eyes.

"It hurts not to cry," I said, half laughing. "I mean,

like my whole face and throat hurts trying to hold it in."

Anna nodded, taking my hand again. "God, do I know *that*."

"You always cry when you want to," I said. "When we first moved here, I'd hear you bawling every night."

Anna looked at me. "But after a while I learned to hold it in. Else I'd always be crying. Always. I hate it here so much . . ." She stopped, shook her head. "This is behind me now. This present is almost over."

"What makes you think it's going to be so much better?"

"Because it already is! Just knowing I won't have to be around us like we are now all bunched up in that stupid tiny apartment, Daddy always at the window looking like some shell and Ma gone crazy with religion! I *hate* us the way—" She stopped again. "It just has to be better, that's all."

"But Mama's got a job now. It'll be different."

Anna looked at me but didn't say anything.

"She's not gonna let you go, you know."

Anna took the envelope off the table and folded the letter back into it. "Yes, she will."

"Jehovah's Witnesses don't believe in college. You're supposed to go into the ministry."

"Jeez, Evie. You're starting to sound like her. You better watch out."

I shrugged. "You have the whole summer to work on her."

Anna shook her head. "The spring semester starts January nineteenth. I have to be there by noon."

"You can't leave in January, Anna."

Anna looked at me and said, "I'm leaving."

The waitress set Anna's tea in front of her and put a check in the middle of the table. Anna put a ten-dollar bill on top of it. "We should give her a nice tip since we probably won't make it to the movies anyway, huh?"

"Whatever."

"Mama's a teacher first, Evie. Even with all the Joho stuff. She wants something better for us than this crap. She hates how we're living. Hates it. You know that and I know that. College? Even as she's trying to argue with me about it, I know she'll be thinking *Yes, this one's getting away!*"

"That was before all of this. She's way different now." I knew I was lying and Anna knew it, too.

She blew on her tea, looking at me over the cup.

"When's your first track meet?"

"Next Saturday. We have to be at school at ten in the morning."

"How come you're not telling them about this?"

"The same reason I didn't tell you. Because it's mine, that's why. And I'm not sure I'm gonna keep running. I don't even know if I'm good at it."

"Who *cares* if you're good at it."

"*I* do. I want to be good at something. I want to be amazing at it. So amazing that nobody's gonna be able to take it away from me."

Anna raised her eyebrows. "Guess we got another movie date coming then, huh, girlie?" She winked at me and took a long sip of her tea.

"Thanks, Anna," I said, meaning it.

22

On Sunday morning, I fell asleep at Kingdom Hall and Mama made me go for a walk when we got home.

"You obviously need some air," she said, annoyed. "If you can't keep your eyes open for a two-hour meeting."

"I'd rather be inside," I lied, and tried not to change too quickly into my running clothes. I winked at Anna as I tied the corny running shoes Mama had bought me, flexing my feet and trying hard not to smile.

It was still cold out, but once I started running, the

air seemed to grow warmer around me. I ran slowly, heading down the block then around the corner toward the park that was a mile from our building. There were people dressed up in church clothes gathered outside the Baptist church near the park and teenagers dressed in party clothes, walking tiredly from the subway. At the entrance to the park, I stopped running and bent over to regain my breath. When I looked up again, I saw Toswiah coming out of the park with a black dog on a leash. She was walking beside a tall girl with glasses and Toswiah's narrow face and high cheekbones. I waved, and the girl lifted her hand and grinned. She walked with a bit of a limp and her left hand lifted into the air. Toswiah tilted her head toward me but didn't wave. I jogged over to them.

"Hey," I said.

"Hey yourself," Toswiah said. "This is my sister. Sheila."

"Hey yourself," Sheila said. She grinned again, then bent down to pet the dog, who was sniffing at me.

Toswiah raised an eyebrow at me but didn't say anything.

"Good doggie," Sheila said. She had a high voice, like someone younger.

"She is a good doggie," I said, bending down to stroke the dog's fur. "I wish I had one."

"You can't have mine!" Sheila said. "She's all mine!" She sat down on the ground and buried her face in the dog's fur.

I looked at Toswiah and smiled. "I really wasn't gonna take her from you guys."

Then Toswiah laughed. "Sheila's kind of attached."

"I see! Jeez, Sheila!"

"All mine," Sheila said, grinning at me.

A wind blew and I shivered. I was sweating underneath the running clothes, and the wind turned the sweat to freezing water on my back. "What's your dog's name?"

"Sheba!" Sheila said. "Sheba and Sheila—forever!"

"You out running?" Toswiah asked.

"No, I'm riding a horse. Of course I'm running!"

Below us, Sheila was making noises at Sheba. The dog lay down, putting its head on Sheila's lap. After a moment, she turned onto her back and let Sheila rub her stomach.

"You a big runner back in San Francisco?" Toswiah asked.

I shrugged. "Kind of."

"I'm gonna go there one day," she said, looking off. "I'm gonna go see me all the great things about San Francisco." She turned to Sheila. "We need to mosey, Sheila."

Sheila got up slowly and wiped off her butt. Sheba looked confused. "I'm gonna go with you!" Sheila said.

Me and Toswiah laughed. I shivered again, then started jogging in place.

"You don't have to go all the way to San Francisco," I said. "I can tell you all about it. Be just like you were there."

Toswiah looked at me, her one eyebrow raised. She stared at me for a long time before she let herself start smiling again. "I'm game to try it that way first. You know—just get my bearings that way before I head on out there." She nodded.

"I'm *cold!*" Sheila said, pulling on Toswiah's arm.

"Then come running with me. That'll warm you up."

Sheila shook her head and grinned. "No. No. No."

"I feel the same way, Sheila," Toswiah said. "See you tomorrow, Evie."

"Yeah," I said, waving and taking off into a run. Behind me, I could feel them standing there watching me. Could feel Toswiah's smiling eyes on my back. I sped up, pumping my arms faster—hearing Leigh's words *Hip to chest with the hands, Spider. Hip to chest.*

My body was fluid. My stride felt flawless. In my head, I saw myself in slow motion, running against the cold wind blowing up all around me. Running *hard* against it, into it, through it. And winning. I, Evie/Toswiah Thomas/Green . . . was winning.

23

THIS MORNING MY FATHER SLAMMED HIS BOWL against the floor, picked up a shard of it and jammed it into his wrist, saying that he was ready to die now. It is Monday. The ambulance came a half hour later, long after Mama had wrapped a towel around his arm, holding him down as he fought against her. Anna and I watched it all without moving, Anna's mouth hanging open, my whole body shaking. There is drying blood by the window. His chair is turned over on its side. We have been standing this way, beside each other, since it happened. My body has stopped shaking but my legs are burning. Now Anna brings his window chair back to the kitchen table. She takes paper towels from the counter, wets them at the sink and starts wiping up the blood. My body is here but my mind isn't. It left as the glass pierced my father's skin.

I am weightless. I am fast. I am free.

PART FOUR

24

THE PRINCIPAL WALKED ON THE STAGE AND asked us—no, she told us to all rise for the Pledge of Allegiance. I stood up and placed my hand over my heart. I said the Pledge at the top of my lungs, every word, just as it's written, clearly and with feeling, the way it's supposed to be said. Then we sang "America the Beautiful" just like we used to do in Denver before all the Joho stuff hit our family. Mama claims we'll have life everlasting if we follow the teachings of her Bible. But you know what? I didn't want life everlasting. I wanted that moment—right there, right then, with everyone's voice lifting up on *America, America. God shed His grace on thee . . .* I wanted *Now.*

Yesterday, I ran into Mira in the hallway.

"Hey Spider," she said. "Where've you been?"

I shrugged. I had missed the first meet. When I left school in the afternoons, I steered clear of the gym. My legs felt heavy these days. Heavy and tight and useless.

"The two hundred," Mira said. "You would have won easily, girl." She smiled, looking puzzled. "No more track for you?"

"Nah," I said. "No more track for me."

"Too bad, Spider. You with all those legs." She turned and headed quickly down the hall, but I just stood there. My legs felt like they weighed a ton. My body felt like it weighed even more than that. Lockers slammed around me. Kids laughed and called out to each other. Someone pushed past me then excused herself. Someone dropped a book and got called a dork for doing it. Soon the hall was empty and still.

At night, long after she's done with her lesson plans, I hear Mama crying. She closes the bathroom door, but the sound leaks through. She turns on the faucet, but her sobs still carry. The doctors say, if things go well, my father will be home in a month or so.

Is he in a straitjacket? I asked my mother that first night.

No, Mama said softly. *Of course not.*

The hospital is named for one of the apostles. The walls are white. The floors are light gray. My father's wrist is bandaged. A physical therapist makes him squeeze a tennis ball to get the use of his fingers back. A psychiatrist asks about his life.

When I visit, my father smiles.

Hey my copper penny, he whispers. *Everything's going to be all right now.*

The medication makes me sleepy, he says. *But it helps me remember who I used to be.*

If the soul is memory, mine has left me. There's tomorrow and the day after, and when I get there, there isn't a yesterday anymore. There is each moment that I spend with Daddy—one more that I almost didn't have.

You run the quarter mile in increments—or splits, as they're called in track—that first curve, the straightaway, another curve, another straightaway, and then you reach the finish line. Before I started running track, I used to think of the quarter as one long race. But it isn't. It's a bunch of little races, split up. Coach calls out your split times and you smile because it was faster than before.

Split by split until the race is over.

IT IS LATE DECEMBER NOW. ANNA IS SAVING up for a suitcase with wheels.

"What about track?" she asks me.

"What about it?" I say.

"It'll free you. That's what."

"Nothing's gonna free me."

"Don't be stupid," Anna says. "Something has to."

"You still planning on going to Simon's Rock?" I ask. Anna nods.

"You don't have to graduate or *anything?*"

"Nope. Just the grades."

I pull my running shoes from our closet then sit on the edge of my bed, staring at them. I think about Mira. I think about Toswiah and her developmentally disabled sister. I think about the way the buildings here go on like mountains, how there are so few green places.

"They take the tiniest plot of land here and plant a tree," I say. "Like, how do they think a tree's gonna grow in that little bit of space? And then, I guess the tree grows, because I see big ones that must have been those stupid little ones one time."

"What are you talking about . . . T?"

I look up at Anna. "I don't know . . . Cam," I whisper. "It just came to my mind."

Anna sits down beside me and touches my face with the back of her hand. I flinch, pull my face away. It seems ridiculous that we're getting closer now. A part of me wants to hit her, hard, ask again how she could even think about leaving. But I don't. Some days I wish Lulu and I had had a huge fight and screamed our hatred at each other. That by the time I left, our friendship had been bruised beyond repair. Then the missing wouldn't hurt so. The holding on wouldn't be so deep.

After a few moments pass, I get up and put the running shoes in my knapsack. It won't free me.

But it's all I have.

25

Two days after New Year's, Coach Leigh
drives us to an outdoor track and tells us to run five
quarters. *All-out*, he says. *Like your life depends on it.*
Like you're running from the bogeyman!

He assigns us lanes and moves to the grassy center
of the field. It is cold out and windy. The track is new
and seems to go on forever.

"It's a quarter-mile track, Evie," Coach Leigh says.
"Once around—all-out."

I stare down the straightaway to where it curves,

then down the back straightaway to where it curves again.

"That back straight's gonna kick our butt in this wind," Mira says. She strides out a few times, jogging back to the group. A few other girls do it, too. I can feel the burn to run in my hamstrings and deep in my throat. The track looks like it can go on and on. Maybe it can.

I am wearing sweats and the racing flats Coach Leigh gave me when I showed up this afternoon.

You planning on staying this time? he asked, holding them away from me. The others looked on, waiting. I had expected people to be crabby, but nobody was.

Yeah, I said.

I can't hear you, Leigh said.

Yeah, I said louder. *Yeah!*

He handed me the running shoes. They are red and white with tiny metal spikes on the bottom.

The rest of your stuff is coming, he said. *Just had to be sure of you first.*

The others are wearing running suits with our school's name on the back. The uniforms are red with white lettering. Beneath the letters, there is a foot with a wing.

When Coach Leigh blows his whistle, we take off, hitting the curve and dropping our shoulders the way he told us to. In the distance, I can hear Coach telling us to relax on the curve. Then he is saying *Pick up the pace* as we round it. I feel myself pulling ahead of the girl in front of me, then Leigh's voice is fading as I move past more girls. In the distance, I can see the Rocky Mountains, Lulu's smiling face, my grandmother holding Matt Cat in her arms.

By the time we hit the final curve, I am back again, the wind leaving me so quickly, my chest feels like it's going to catch on fire. I can hear Leigh cheering, hear the others breathing hard behind me, hear our feet moving like two big feet—in unison, connected. When I get to the finish line, I can see my father, standing there with his bandaged arm and hospital gown. And beside him—two girls—Evie and Toswiah, blurring into each other. I want to keep running, past these ghosts, past everyone and everything, but there isn't any more air left in me. Just a sadness. Newer than before. And deep as everything.

"Spider!" Mira grins between deep gulps of air. She

bends over and puts her hands on her knees. "You run pretty fast, but that's the last time you'll ever beat me."

We jog slowly, Mira keeping a few steps ahead of me. I can see Leigh, standing in the center, grinning.

Some girls jog past us, saying "Good running," and slap me on the butt.

"Don't listen to them," Mira says, turning around and jogging backward. "They're just like me—planning how to catch you next time!" She picks up her pace a bit and the other girls follow her. But I hang back, still catching my breath.

"Catch up to them, Spider," Coach Leigh yells. "You got four more quarters to run."

26

EVIE IVIE OVER. HERE COMES A TEACHER WITH A BIG fat stick. I wonder what she's got for arithmetic! One and one? Two! Me and you. Who?

Sometimes I look at the girl sitting next to me in class and wonder what her secrets are. Maybe there are others in class like me. In this room. All over the world. Outside, it rains and rains. Our teacher is going on about the impact of air on blood—how the air changes it from blue to red. I want to raise my hand and ask, "Who would I be in an airless, empty room?"

But I don't. And never will.

This morning on the radio a singer was asking her lover if he liked either or both of her. When I heard that line, I stopped brushing my hair and moved closer to the radio. The singer went on about how she's different people at different times and kept coming back to the refrain—"Do you like or love either or both of me?" I stood in my bedroom listening to the song, feeling a smile coming on. I am Toswiah Green. I am Evie Thomas. And some days I like and love either and both of me.

Carlos, who sits directly in front of me, turns now and makes a face, then smiles. I look at him but don't smile back, then, after a moment, I do. He puts a chocolate kiss on my desk and turns back around. When I pull the candy toward me, it is soft, already melting. Maybe my cooties are fading. The teacher's voice changes and then she is talking about our hearts, how amazing they are, what all they do to keep us living. I press my hand to my chest. Seven months have passed since we left Denver in the middle of the night. My heart is still beating. I am no longer who I was in Denver, but at least and at most—I *am*.

27

MAMA SITS AT THE KITCHEN TABLE, READING the letter slowly, again and again, while Anna stands beside her, her arms folded, her bottom lip pulled beneath her teeth. It is Saturday morning. Outside, snow is falling. A thin layer of it is already on the ground. Our apartment and the world outside are silent. Downstairs, new neighbors are moving in. I have pulled my father's chair back to the window and now watch a little girl skip from the moving truck to our front stairs. She looks up at the window and waves, then holds her dolls up for me to see. I wave back, press my face to the window and wait for Mama to start yelling.

"I'm going, Mama," Anna says.

The little girl's mother is carrying a stack of framed pictures. She steps carefully across the snow. She is tall and young-looking. When she looks up at the window, she smiles. Downstairs I can hear doors opening and closing. The little girl lets out a laugh now that fills the hallway. She has a sweet laugh. For over a year, we've been the only ones in this building.

On the mantelpiece, there is a Polaroid of me and Anna. We have our foreheads pressed together so that the picture is only of our profiles. But Anna is looking at the camera—sideways. I am looking at Anna and laughing. The picture is blurred because Anna held the camera in her own hand to take it. *Too close,* she said after it developed. But the blur is fine to me. That's who we are here—ourselves, but just a little different.

When Mama looks up from the letter, I close my eyes. *Please, God.*

"I'm going," Anna says again, her voice a little shakier than before.

"Of course you are," Mama says. "Of course you are."

Anna looks at me, then back at Mama, then at me again and smiles.

Now there are tears in Mama's eyes. Tears that she wipes away quickly. When she stands, it is not to tear the letter into a million pieces and fuss at Anna about forging names, but to hug her, hug her hard and cry.

Who would I be in an airless room? Who am I now? A bug on the wall. Today I am the younger daughter. The quieter one. The one who will stay a while longer. Today I am Spider, Hey Evie, what's up?, Daddy Longlegs, Ms. Thomas. Daddy's daughter. A child of God. Silly. Pretty. Skinny. Some of these things—I'll still be tomorrow.

In the hallway, I can hear the little girl singing *Hush, little baby, don't say a word. Daddy's gonna buy you a mockingbird. . . .*

I raise the window a bit and stick my hand out. The snow melts as quickly as it touches me. Outside, the little girl twirls and twirls, holding her dolls high up. *And if that mockingbird don't sing,* I whisper along with her. *Daddy's gonna buy you a diamond ring. . . .*

28

My father peels back the bandages to show me the scar running from his wrist to the crook of his arm. I close my eyes for a moment, resting my forehead against his shoulder.

"Daddy . . ."

"It's all right now, my copper penny," he says. "I'm here. I was gone for a while, but I'm here now."

He presses the bandages back in place and holds his arm up as we walk to the dayroom. When people pass us, I try not to stare. I want to see crazy close-up, though. Understand this thing that Anna says our father is. Because if it's in him, it's in me. His craziness—my inheritance. Some of the people shuffle when they walk, their heads hanging down. But the few people who pass us look regular, like anyone walking down the street—their backs straight, their steps as sure as mine. The hallways here are painted white and smell like medicine and pine cleaner. Muffled voices drift out of the rooms on either side of us. Otherwise, it is quiet. So much quiet in such a big space. When I look at my father's face, the quiet is there, too—no, not quiet maybe. Something else. Peace.

At the end of the hall, there is a solarium. Ceiling-to-floor windows and plants everywhere. The room feels like springtime. Outside, though, the sky is gray. My father nods at a couple of people. They are dressed as he is—in loose-fitting sweats and pull-on sneakers.

"Hey Evan," a pretty nurse says. "Is this one of the daughters?"

My father smiles and introduces me. I move a step closer to him, holding on to his good arm. Feeling proud to be one of his daughters, even here. I am nearly as tall as he is. Maybe this happened a long time ago.

We find wicker chairs by the windows and sit facing each other. My father looks at me for a long time, his gaze so intense, I look away, bend to scratch my ankle even though it's not itching.

"Doctor says the surgery was successful," he says. He holds his arm out and makes a fist. The bandages are as white as the walls. "The bowl went . . . went through some nerves when I did what I did." He looks off, away from me. "I'm glad I'm here now."

"Yeah?"

He looks at me and smiles. "Yeah."

"Are you glad you're alive?"

For the quickest moment, his face crumbles, but he catches it and nods. "I am *so* glad I'm alive, Evie. So glad we all are."

We get quiet again. At practice, Coach tells us to run for our lives. One day I might tell him that I've already done that, watch his face get that puzzled look it gets when one of us makes a crack that he doesn't understand. *My whole family, Coach*, I might say. *We're all runners.*

"You have every right to be mad," my father says now.

"I'm not mad."

"How could you not be, Evie? You have so many things to be mad about."

"Like us leaving Denver?"

My father nods. "Us leaving Denver. Coming here." He holds up his bandaged arm. "This."

I stare down at my hands. I wasn't mad. I couldn't be. All this time I'd been thinking about all the stuff we'd lost—our friends, Grandma, our names, some stupid old clothes. But my father—he'd lost everything. Everything he'd ever known. The morning the lieutenant pinned that medal to his chest, Daddy had looked over at us and grinned. Grinned like the world was complete. Like he had found perfection.

"You wanted to save our lives," I say finally.

"That's what *I* wanted," my father says. "But what about what *you* wanted, Evie?" He looks around the solarium, takes a deep breath.

I shrug. "It goes somewhere, Daddy. It goes out of me. I used to be mad about everything. I used to hate this place and all the people in it. I'd stand in the middle of the school yard and just . . . just shut every single part of me . . . off."

I lean closer to him, gently touch his bandages. I

want to ask him about right and wrong. When do you know what's what. I want to believe he did the right thing. When we were little, my grandmother used to always say *In all your getting, get understanding.* I want to get understanding now.

There is soft music being piped in around us. Daddy listens to it for a moment, his eyes closed, his head moving the tiniest bit.

"I don't know what I want, Daddy. Not yet. Not anymore. I have some new ideas, though. Big Evie Thomas ideas."

Coach Leigh says he thinks I'm gonna break records one day. He says my running reminds him of some of the greatest quarter-milers that ever hit the track. *You got a lot of practice ahead of you,* he says, smiling. *And a lot of promise, Spider.* When he says this, I get a feeling so deep—like I can do anything. There is a fire inside of me. It burns and burns.

Anna says she believes there's a reason for everything that happens—even us coming here. Some mornings I think about what Lulu used to say about God having set our stage long before we were even in this world. I think about my own stage—how in the middle of the play, God said *Cut!*

I think in the middle of everything, God changed His mind. And, maybe, just maybe, came up with a better idea.

I smile and take my father's hand, thinking *My life is a rewrite. I hope this is the last revision.*

"Daddy," I say, "tell me about when you first knew you wanted to be a cop."

My father looks at me. He seems confused for a moment, but then his smile comes. Slowly. But it comes. The old smile. Daddy's smile. It creeps up from his face like all those memories of our days before here and all those sweet promises—*a lot of promise*—of what's ahead of us.

Me and Daddy stare at each other for a long time—two old, old buddies who knew each other when . . .

ACKNOWLEDGMENTS

Thanks so much to all the people who read this in its many stages and gave me amazing feedback, including Juliet Widoff, Toshi Reagon, Catherine Gund, Jill Harris, Catherine Mckinley, Gloria Fisk, Stacey D'Erasmo, Stephanie Grant, Teresa Calabrese, and Nancy Paulsen.

And thanks to Linda Villarosa for helping me with research.

QUESTIONS FOR DISCUSSION

- Describe Evie's life in Denver before her father witnessed the shooting. Why is her real name so important to her?

- How did her mother become involved with religion? Why?

- Why does Evie's grandmother refuse to leave Denver?

- Why is it so important for Evie's father to testify in this case? What other actions could he have taken?

- Contrast Evie's home in Denver with her family's new home.

- Each member of the family leaves something important behind when they are forced to leave Denver. Describe what each leaves behind and why it matters.

- Why does Evie decide to join the track team and why does she keep it a secret?

- Anna decides to try to gain admittance to a college that will accept her before she graduates. Why is this important to her? What impact will this have on her family? On Evie?

- How are Evie and her father able to reach each other again? What understanding does Evie gain when she is able to finally speak openly with her father again?

Turn the page for a sample
of **JACQUELINE WOODSON**'s

After Tupac
and D Foster

The summer before D Foster's real mama came and took her away, Tupac wasn't dead yet. He'd been shot five times—two in the head, two down by his leg and thing and one shot that went in his hand and came out the other side and went through a vein or something. All the doctors were saying he should have died and were bringing other doctors up to his room to show everybody what a medical miracle he was. That's what they called him. A Medical Miracle. Like he wasn't even a real person. Like he was just something to be looked at and turned this way and that way and poked at. Like he wasn't Tupac.

D Foster showed up a few months before Tupac got shot that first time and left us the summer before he died. By the time her mama came and got her and she took one last walk on out of our lives, I felt like we'd grown up and grown old and lived a hundred lives in those few years that we knew her. But we hadn't really. We'd just gone from being eleven to being thirteen. Three girls. Three the Hard Way. In the end, it was just me and Neeka again.

The first time Tupac got shot, it was November 1994. Cold as anything everywhere in the city and me, Neeka, D and everybody else was shivering our behinds through the winter with nobody thinking Pac was gonna make it. Then, right after he had some surgery, he checked himself out of the hospital even though the doctors was trying to tell him he wasn't well enough to be doing that. That's when everybody around here started talking about what a true gangsta he was. At least that's what all the kids were thinking. The churchgoing people just kept saying he had God with him. Some of the parents were saying what they'd always been saying about him—that he was heading right to what he got because he was a bad example for kids, especially black kids like us. Crazy stuff about Tupac being a disgrace to the race and blah, blah, blah. The wannabe gangsta kids just kept saying Tupac was gonna get revenge on whoever did that to him.

2

But when I saw Tupac like that—coming out of the hospital, all skinny and small-looking in that wheelchair, big guards around him—I remember thinking, *He ain't gonna try to get revenge on nobody and he ain't trying to be a disgrace to anybody either. Just trying to keep on.* Even though he wasn't smiling, I knew he was just happy and confused about still being alive.

Went on like that all winter long, then February came and they sent Tupac to jail for some dumb stuff and people started talking about that—the negative peeps talking about that's where he needed to be and all the rest of us saying how messed up the law was when you didn't look and act like people thought you should.

Spring came and Pac dropped his album from prison and this one song on it was real tight, so we all just listened to it and talked about how bad-ass Pac was—that he wasn't even gonna let being in jail stop him from making his music. Me and Neeka and D had all turned twelve by then, but we still believed stuff—like that we'd grow up and marry beautiful rapper guys who'd buy us huge houses out in the country. We talked about how they'd be all crazy over us and if some other girl walked by who was fine or something, they wouldn't even turn their heads to look because they'd be so in love with us and all. Stupid stuff like that.

In jail, Pac started getting clear about thug life, saying it wasn't the right thing. He got all *righteous* about it and whatnot, and with all the rappers shooting on each other and stuff, it wasn't hard to agree with him.

Time kept passing on that way. Things and people changing. First, D turned thirteen, then me and Neeka were right
there behind her—us all turning into teenagers, getting body,
getting tall, boys acting stupid over us.

Seems soon as we started settling into all that changing,
D's mama came—took her away from us.

And time kept on creeping.

Then Tupac went and died and it got me thinking about
D. About the short time she was with us and about how you
could know somebody real good but not know them at the
same time. And it made me want to remember. Yeah, I guess
that's it. I guess that's what I'm trying to do now. . . .

PART
ONE

Maybe, while he was in jail, Tupac started thinking about his Big Purpose. That's what D called it—our Big Purpose. She said everybody's got one and it's just that we gotta figure out what it is and then go have it.

The night she said it for the first time, it was late in the summer 1995 and we were all just hanging out—me, her and Neeka—watching music videos on TV. Before they started coming on regular, we'd have to watch the bootleg copies and sometimes those were so bad, we could hardly see the people in them. If it was a Tupac video, the only thing all the girls wanted to see real good was Tupac's eyes. He had the prettiest eyes of any rapper—they were all big and sad-looking and he had dark eyebrows that were so thick, they made you think about soft things.

That night, they showed "Brenda's Got A Baby," one of Tupac's old videos where Tupac sang about the young girl getting pregnant, and in the video Tupac was holding the baby because Brenda had put it in a garbage can. Me, Neeka and D was sitting on the floor in my living room. We'd put our money together and had enough for a small pizza and a liter of Pepsi. With a small pie, everybody could have at least two slices. D hadn't eaten anything since school lunch, so her eyes got real wide when she realized how much we had.

"Dag, my girls!" she said, her smile getting all big. "We gonna eat like we stupid tonight!"

And we did. We'd each had our two slices and were working on the last two, passing the slices back and forth between us—me taking a bite, then passing it to Neeka, Neeka taking a bite, then passing it on to D. D had the slice when Tupac's video came on.

"They don't hardly never be playing Pac," she said. "It's like they scared of him or something."

It was dark in the living room except for the blue light

coming off the screen. D got real quiet and stopped eating. I could see the shiny line of pizza grease moving past her bony wrist and on down her arm.

"Hey D," Neeka said. "You babysitting that slice? Pass it on, girl."

But D just kept staring at the TV like she couldn't hear anymore, holding the slice up, frozen in midair.

"Forget about it," I said. "I'm done anyway."

I leaned back against the couch. Tupac's beautiful eyes came up close on the screen. His mouth moved slowly as he sang about Brenda never ever really having a chance in life. His eyes looked sad like he was really singing about the truth and somebody he knew real good. Maybe he was thinking about his own mama—how she'd been in jail when she was pregnant with him. Not because she'd done something real wrong or anything—just because she was in this militant group, the Black Panthers. Back in the day, the Black Panthers were always marching and trying to get things changed so that black people could live a little bit better—like they're the reason there was free breakfast in school and stuff like that. Tupac's mama had gotten arrested and when she went to jail, she started making changes there—making sure pregnant women had decent food so that their babies could be born healthy and all. Everybody who knew Tupac knew about his mama. He loved her more than anything. Maybe Tupac was singing

about Brenda but really thinking about his own mama—
how she could have just thrown him away but she didn't.
Instead, she made sure he was born healthy. And strong.

"Him and me," D said, real quiet. "It's like we the same in
some crazy way."

Neeka looked at me and made a face.

"The only way you and him's the same," Neeka said, "is
that you both Nee-groes. But you broke-ass and Tupac's got
some money in his pockets."

D kept staring at the TV. Tupac was walking slow with
his boys all around. His head down. He was so beautiful, I
felt like I could see Brenda inside of him. Like even though
he was singing about a girl who threw her baby away, he was
thinking about himself. Made me wonder if he was seeing
himself as Brenda or the baby.

"It's like I look at him and I see myself. It's like I'm
looking in a mirror," D said. She turned to the pizza slice
she was holding, like she was just remembering it was there,
then reached past Neeka. "Here," she said, handing it to me.
"I'm full."

"Me too," I said, pushing the slice back at her. She dropped
it into the empty pizza box, then took a napkin and wiped
the oil off her arm.

"You should just rub that in," Neeka said. "Your arm's all ashy."

"You hush!" D said. But she was smiling.

"You still ain't tell me what else you got in common with
Tupac," Neeka said.

"Was your mama in jail like his mama?" I asked.

D shook her head. She curled her fingers into her palm and stared down at them.

"My mama is somewhere being somebody's hot mess."

She got quiet for a minute. "He sings about things that I'm living, you know. When he be singing the 'Dear Mama' song, that makes me think about my own mama. It's like his mama was a mess sometimes and he still loved her—people's moms be all complicated, and it's not like you got a bad mama or you got a good mama the way people be trying to judge and say."

D smiled.

"It's like he sees stuff, you know? And he *knows* stuff. And he be thinking stuff that only somebody who knows that kinda living deep and true could know and think."

"Yeah," Neeka said. "And he gets paid big dollars for those thoughts. That's way, way, *way* different from us."

The Tupac video went off and Public Enemy came on. I couldn't stand PE with their stupid big clocks around their necks and all that military stuff. It didn't make any sense to me.

Neeka and D didn't like them either. I turned the sound down.

"Y'all spending the night?" I asked.

Neeka nodded but D shook her head.

"Flo said she'd beat my behind if I didn't come home." She got up off the floor. Her foster mom's name wasn't Flo, we just called her that. Short for Foster Lady Orderly. It was real late for D to be taking the bus back to Flo's house. She started putting on her sandals and getting her stuff together. We'd been friends for almost a year but we'd never seen where she lived.

"We gonna walk you to the bus stop," I said, getting up off the couch. "C'mon, Neeka."

"You sure lucky," D said to Neeka.

"For what?" Neeka stretched real high and yawned, her skinny brown belly showing out from under her T-shirt.

"Just 'cause you get to spend the night." D took a brush out of her pocketbook and brushed her hair. It was straightened, but Flo wouldn't let her wear any styles except two cornrows or a whole lot of box braids. Whenever D got around our way, she took the cornrows out and just let her hair be free. But she always remembered to put it back like it was before she got on the bus.

"You should just tell the crazy lady you almost grown," Neeka said. "And then come around here and let me hook you up with some fly hair and some good fashion."

D stopped brushing. I clicked the TV off and turned on the light. We all squinted against the brightness.

"Dag, girl," Neeka said. "Give a sister a warning before you turn on a light."

"Why you always gotta say that, Neeka?" D was pointing the brush at her.

"Say what?"

"Tell me to go tell Flo about herself."

"'Cause you *should*."

"And then what?" D looked mad now. Her eyes were dark green—pretty in a strange way, like they should have been on somebody different but at the same time looking like they almost belonged to her. Her skin wasn't brown like mine or light brown like Neeka's—it was kinda *tan* brown in that way that made people always ask her what she was mixed with. When she said, "I'm half black and half your mama!" me and Neeka would laugh and the person would either get mad or laugh too. D hated people asking what she was. Maybe because she didn't know who her daddy was.

Neeka rolled her eyes. "If you told Flo to kiss your butt, she'd see you was half grown and stop treating you like some-body's baby."

"Last I heard, twelve wasn't half grown—"

"In six years, you'll be eighteen," Neeka said. "You eigh-teen, you legal."

"If I *make it* to eighteen. If I don't act right, I'm out of the system and on my own. And probably *homeless*. I been in the system long enough to see how jacked up it is. Kids living in the streets because they couldn't get along with their foster mamas. Kids all caught out there and whatnot. I am *so* not trying to go down like that." D put the brush in her bag and started braiding, her hands flying through her hair like she'd been braiding it for a hundred years.